Reid's voice was deep, husky and so gentle it brought sudden scalding tears to her eyes, and Joanna was filled with a breathless, poignant yearning for what she'd lost. At this moment, he was the old Reid, the man she'd fallen in love with.

Grimly, she shook her head. "No! We have to go through with it."

He looked skeptical. "She'll see right through you."

"Don't worry about me. I can put on an act just as well as you can." She reached out and ran her hands over his chest, feeling the warmth of his body beneath the fine cotton of his shirt.

He started in surprise as she leaned up to him and whispered, "Till next Friday, darling."

Something hot and dark flared in his eyes, just before she covered his mouth with her own. Insistently, she slid her tongue along his lips until his mouth opened. Her senses were flooded with the warmth of him, the scent of him, as his tongue languorously entwined with hers. Her whole body burned for him.

But then his hands slid up to grasp her arms and he broke the kiss. Abruptly, she pushed away from him with trembling hands and looked him in the face. "Was that sufficiently wifely?"

Debra Carroll is really two people: Carol Bruce-Thomas and Debra McCarthy-Anderson. Friends forever, the pair decided they wanted to do something new and interesting with their lives. Rather like Mickey Rooney to Judy Garland, one said to the other, "I know, let's write a romance!" They set a five-year goal to sell to Harlequin. Along the way they published two romance novels under the name of Rachel Vincer with Meteor Books. And then, with only days to spare in the five-year deadline, Harlequin phoned and offered them a contract. *An Inconvenient Passion* is their fourth book for Temptation. Look for many more sizzling stories from this dynamic duo!

Books by Debra Carroll

HARLEQUIN TEMPTATION
526—OBSESSION
568—MAN UNDER THE MISTLETOE
578—TO CATCH A THIEF

AN INCONVENIENT PASSION
Debra Carroll

Harlequin Books

TORONTO • NEW YORK • LONDON
AMSTERDAM • PARIS • SYDNEY • HAMBURG
STOCKHOLM • ATHENS • TOKYO • MILAN
MADRID • WARSAW • BUDAPEST • AUCKLAND

ISBN 0-373-25697-3

AN INCONVENIENT PASSION

Copyright © 1996 by Carol Bruce-Thomas and
Debra McCarthy-Anderson.

Printed in U.S.A.

Prologue

JOANNA CURSED under her breath, yanking hard on the steering wheel. Over the loud pounding of her heart, she heard tires screaming as the back end of the Porsche shot out sideways on the icy road. The car lurched into the circular driveway of the old mansion, barely missing the first of the giant oaks lining the drive.

A quick glance in the rearview mirror showed the car behind slewing heavily around the abrupt turn. She expelled her breath in a hiss of exasperation. At least he'd shut off that damn siren.

Jamming her foot on the brake, she brought the car to a skidding halt on the snowy gravel. Barely waiting for the vehicle to come to a stop, she opened the door and stumbled out, slammed the door behind her and broke into a run. The heavy thunk followed her, reverberating in the sudden silence of an icy February morning.

A large hand, clamped down heavily on her shoulder, and brought her to a sudden stop. "Hey you," came a surly growl. "Where do you think you're going?"

The chill cut through her inadequate clothing and she turned, shivering and impatient, to confront the large, sandy-haired and very angry man in blue.

"For heaven's sake, leave me alone! Can't you see I'm in a hurry?"

"Yeah, I can see that all right. In case you didn't know, lady, it's against the law to be in that much of a hurry." He planted himself solidly in her way and reached into his breast pocket.

"So give me a ticket...."

"Hey, don't get smart with me. That's exactly what I'm goin' to do." With infuriating slowness, he pulled out his ticket book and flipped it open.

"Good! Now get out of my way. This is an emergency." She darted past him. He made a grab for her, but missed as she bolted toward the door.

"I'll need your license—" he yelled after her, with a belligerence that told her this would be expensive. As if she cared right now.

"In the glove compartment," she tossed back over her shoulder, her footsteps crunching loudly on the frozen gravel as she dashed up the shallow marble steps.

Behind the glass of the Victorian double doors stood a middle-aged woman dressed in crisp white. A stranger, not one of the daytimers. She had barely unlocked the door when Joanna burst through.

"Is she still—?" Joanna had to pause for a moment to gulp some air into her burning lungs and try to get her labored breathing under control. "Is she still with us?"

The woman nodded. "Yes." But her curious gaze was on the scene outside.

Joanna took a quick look over her shoulder and saw the policeman's broad butt sticking out of the cramped interior of her car.

She grimaced, clutching at the sharp stitch in her side. "You might say I burned a little rubber getting here."

"I see." The woman reached around her to close the door on the cold draft, then her gaze traveled over Joanna and a small sympathetic smile curved her thin lips.

Glancing down, Joanna noticed that her camel's hair coat hung open, revealing the blue-striped pajamas underneath, hastily shoved into tall leather boots.

"I didn't want to waste time changing." She looked a sight, but right now that didn't matter.

She stepped quickly past the woman in white, flew across the circular foyer to the broad staircase and started up the stairs two at a time.

Every nerve tingled with vibrant awareness, but she felt weirdly disoriented, as if she'd been jolted back to life, not merely awakened from a sound sleep half an hour before.

"When did this happen?" she asked breathlessly as she dashed toward the second floor with the woman at her heels, the old wooden stairs creaking softly at every step.

"I'm not really sure. I found her like this at four-thirty." The woman, panting in the effort to keep up, kept her voice low. "The last time I checked, when I turned her at two-thirty, Mrs. Clooney was just as usual."

As Joanna reached the top of the stairs and started down the hall the silence of the big house descended, broken only by the soft padding of her boots and the barely audible squeak of the white oxfords behind her. She walked quickly down the short corridor, toward a broad bay window that let in the pale light of dawn, and stopped at the white-painted door at the end.

"Now, I want you to be prepared." Concern filled the other woman's kindly face. "Don't be alarmed if she doesn't know you or seem to respond to you. That'll all take time."

"I understand."

Squeezing her eyes shut, Joanna dragged in a deep breath to calm her nerves, vibrating with tension like bowstrings.

"Would you like me to come in with you?"

The woman's gentle solicitude was touching, but Joanna shook her head. "No . . . I'll be all right."

"Okay, I'll be here if you need me, and Dr. Malcho is on her way."

"Thank you." Joanna's throat felt so dry she could barely swallow as she put a trembling hand against the door and slowly pushed it open.

Bathed in the peach light of the rising sun, the familiar room looked suddenly strange and new. But all she really saw was the woman propped up in the raised bed, small and frail in her crisp white cotton nightdress, her pale face framed by short, fashionably cut ash-blond hair.

She was the same, no different from the person who'd been lying there in a deep sleep day after day, month after endless month. Her eyes were closed, her thin, beautifully manicured hands resting unmovingly on the cotton blanket.

But now her eyes fluttered open and slowly turned toward the door. And for the first time in three years Joanna looked into the pale green eyes that watched her in confused awareness. Tears blurred her vision and burned her throat as she looked at the fragile woman in the bed.

A strangled sob tore from her, and she covered her mouth with one badly shaking hand. Then she ran across the room to enfold the small body in her arms.

"Momma," she choked out.

Her mother lay limp and quiescent in her arms as Joanna blinked away the hot tears that welled in her eyes. "I thought you were never coming back...I thought you were gone forever...."

Swallowing hard past the painful lump in her throat she managed a weak smile, but her wobbly voice betrayed her. "I've missed you so much."

She buried her face in her mother's lap to hide her burning eyes. It would be so easy to give in and weep, allow the tears to wash away the legacy of pain and fear.

All these months her mother had lain there, dead to the world around her. And now to have her back.... She had to be calm, but it was almost beyond her.

1

"WHERE'S REID?" asked Louise Clooney in a shaky whisper.

Joanna felt the blood drain from her face in shock. After ten weeks of therapy, her mother had finally spoken. Joanna had been waiting anxiously for these first precious words and now she could only stare in dumb horror. It had never occurred to her for a moment that her mother would ask for him.

"He's ... he's ..." She gasped like a drowning victim going under for the third time and shot an alarmed look at Dr. Malcho.

The older woman was just removing the blood-pressure cuff from her patient's arm. The doctor's keen gray eyes watched her curiously from behind steel-rimmed glasses.

Joanna licked her dry lips and evaded the question. "You shouldn't have any other visitors, not yet. Not till you're stronger."

"I ... want ... to see him." With enormous effort her mother jerkily formed the words, then slumped back onto the plumply cushioned wing chair and closed her eyes.

"As soon as you're a little stronger," Joanna croaked, panic rising up to choke her.

She shook her head restlessly against the padded chair back and her breathing became labored. "No. Now."

"But Mom, the doctor's orders . . ."

"Please . . . Joanna." Every word cost her so much that it was painful to watch. "Bring . . . Reid . . . to see me."

"He's . . . he's out of town," she said desperately, "on business."

The green eyes fluttered open and fastened on her. "When will he be back?"

It was impossible to meet her mother's tired gaze. "Not for a few weeks," she said wildly.

The pale mouth tightened. Clearly unsatisfied, she sank back on the cushions in apparent exhaustion.

"Come along now, Joanna. My patient needs her rest." The doctor quickly ushered her out of the room into the corridor of the private hospital and shut the door behind them.

Joanna slumped back against the wall and lowered her head into her hands with a groan. "Why didn't I anticipate this?"

"Anticipate what?" The doctor asked briskly. "Who's Reid?"

"Reid O'Connor. You've probably seen him. I know he comes to visit my mother from time to time."

"Of course—Mr. O'Connor. Yes, he does come in now and then." She smiled. "He talks to her, sometimes he even sings to her. As a matter of fact, the last time he came in was just before she woke up."

"He's my ex-husband. We separated a couple of months after her accident. She's going to be terribly upset when she finds out."

"They had a close relationship?"

"Close!" Joanna shuddered. "She adored Reid." She felt cold despair numbing her brain. "Telling her about Dad was terrifying. How can I tell her about Reid too?"

Dr. Malcho's kindly face filled with concern. "I wish I had an answer."

"Yes, so do I." Joanna closed her eyes against the horror of the situation. "This is too much." The words burst out of her, low and impassioned. "I can't handle any more."

The doctor took her hand in a firm grip, her manner stern yet sympathetic. "I know this hasn't been easy for you, but you've got to be strong now, as you have been all along. You can do it."

Joanna gave a wry grimace. "Yeah, I know I can do it. I have to. I have no choice. But how am I going to tell her about Reid?"

The news of her father's death had hit her mother with devastating impact. Despondent and listless from grief, she'd completely given up trying to get better. For weeks she'd made no effort with the physical therapy that would eventually help her walk again, and had virtually ignored the speech pathologist.

All through that hellish time Joanna had worried herself sick, terrified that one day she'd come in and find her mother gone again, this time for good.

No. She'd sooner die than add to her anguish.

"I can't tell her the truth, but how can I lie to her about something so important?"

"I can see your dilemma." The doctor's warm gray eyes became grave and Joanna looked away from the older woman's sympathy. She didn't want sympathy. What she wanted was a solution.

For a moment she had the wicked thought that things would be so much simpler if the coma had caused her mother to forget Reid's existence. Fat chance of that. Reid was a hard man to forget.

It had been three years since she'd left him, but *she* hadn't forgotten, not one single detail of their life together.

Oh, she'd shoved him to the back of her memory—at least she'd tried. And definitely over the past few months she'd succeeded in forgetting about everything and everybody except her mother.

But now the thought of him brought the painful, familiar knowledge that where Reid was concerned, nothing had changed. He'd washed his hands of her, and now they were like two strangers.

Taking another deep breath, she pushed the pain aside and rallied her strength. This wasn't about *her* feelings. They didn't matter right now. What mattered was that woman on the other side of the door.

She'd bought herself some time, but eventually she'd have to either produce a husband or tell her mother the truth. The enormity of the situation made her feel overwhelmed and helpless.

She had no answers, no idea what to do. It would be so comfortable right now just to slip into a coma herself, and leave someone else to sort out the mess.

WHEN THE SUBJECT came up again, ten days later, her mother's voice was noticeably stronger, her speech more firm.

"When did you say Reid will be back?" she asked, hanging on to the walker as she gingerly sank down into the wing chair by the window.

Joanna restrained the automatic urge to take her mother's arm and help. Louise Clooney was only forty-eight years old, but it was hard to remember the active woman she had been before the car accident that had put her in a coma.

"In a week. I . . . I'm just not exactly sure what day." She stumbled over the words, her brain in a frantic whirl.

"Call him. Tell him I want to see him."

Her mother pushed the walker to one side and Joanna sat down in the matching chair, facing her across a small table where tea things were set out.

"I can't do that, Mom. He sends his love." Her stomach rolled again. Talk about digging yourself in deeper.

She picked up the teapot and leaned over to pour the tea, steadying the pot with her left hand.

"Where's your wedding ring?"

Joanna looked up to find her peering closely at the ten-carat diamond on her ring finger. Paul's ring. My God, she'd forgotten she was wearing it!

She put the pot down hastily, mumbling something about it being too hot and clasped her hands together to cover the glittering jewel. "I, uh, took my ring off to clean it and I forgot to put it back on."

"That's not your engagement ring. What happened to your ring?"

"I . . . I lost it . . . a while back." Her fingers found the ring and began twisting it nervously. "I, uh, replaced it with this one."

"Reid must be doing very well to afford a rock like that." Her mother smiled with tired contentment. "I'm so glad. He deserves it. I'm very fond of Reid, you know." The shrewd, penetrating eyes were hard to meet.

"Yes, I know, Mom," Joanna mumbled.

"Things have gone well for you two?"

"Yes, very well," she answered faintly, sinking further into the quicksand of lies. But what could she do?

"Good." Her mother smiled and gave a weak nod of satisfaction. What little energy she had was still quickly drained by the physical therapy, but she *was* making progress. "I have to admit for a while there at the beginning I was a little worried about you two. But I can see that you've worked everything out."

"Yes, we worked everything out," Joanna repeated faintly, feeling the last drop of blood draining from her face.

"The important thing is that you love each other. When you love each other, everything can be worked out. But I know very well how difficult the first couple of years of marriage can be. I remember when your father and I were starting out." She sighed. "It was very rocky...."

Joanna had ceased to listen as her mind revolved in horrified circles. What was she going to do?

With a click, the door opened and the evening nurse stepped in. "Okay you two, break it up, visiting hours are over."

"Oh, Sally, we can visit another few minutes, surely?" Her mother sweetly implored the young nurse. "We haven't had our tea."

Sally gave her a warm smile. "Oh, I guess so. You know how to get around me."

Joanna had been amused at the speed and ease with which her mother had charmed the nursing staff and had them all eating out of the palm of her hand. Even in this weakened state, her warmth drew people to her. She had the endearing habit of taking those she liked instantly to her heart. But right now that thought didn't warm Joanna one bit.

That was exactly how she had reacted to Reid. As soon as she'd discovered that his own parents were both dead, she'd taken him under her wing and he'd responded to her maternal treatment. They had a special bond, more like mother and son than son-in-law.

That was what made it impossible to tell her mother that the marriage was over, why she found herself lying to her own mother. But how could she get out of it when the only alternative was the truth?

Right now she needed to be alone to do some thinking.

She shot to her feet. "Oh no, Sally's right, you need your rest. I'll come back tomorrow."

"Bring my son-in-law with you." Her mother closed her eyes and leaned her head back. "I want to see him."

She was so thin that she was almost swallowed up by the high-backed chair. Her skin looked paper-white above the smart blue dress. Joanna felt her heart tighten with pain to see how the ravages of illness and grief had deepened the lines on her mother's face. She looked twenty years older than her actual age.

All that night Joanna lay awake, worrying until her head spun. Over and over she asked herself *What am I going to do?*

She was utterly sick of the question, but she had no answer. Except that she absolutely could not tell that frail woman about the divorce.

And then, in the small hours of the morning, an idea began to germinate in her mind. It was crazy, but it was the only solution. There was only one little problem: would Reid go for it?

LUCKILY THERE WAS a free parking spot right in front of the neo-Georgian townhouse. Joanna emerged from the car, then stood on the pavement for a moment, looking up at the tall, narrow facade.

Reid's was the end unit of a row of renovated, restored and very upscale downtown homes, tucked away on an exclusive side street in the heart of Toronto. Only a discreet brass plaque on the door with the words, R.

O'Connor Ltd., indicated that this was also a place of business.

With hands that felt cold and clammy, she turned the handle and walked in. Reid's business was devoted to building and remodeling one-of-a-kind houses, and a quick glance showed that the interior was as superbly restored as the facade. The whole ground floor had been opened up into a combined studio and office space.

A state-of-the-art computer system hummed softly on one of the desks and toward the back a drafting table caught the light from a wall of windows looking out on to a tiny, perfect city garden.

"May I help you?" A dark-haired woman, very attractive and coolly professional, rose from one of the desks. She looked to be in her early thirties, around the same age as Reid, Joanna noted absently.

"I'm here to see Mr. O'Connor," she said, feeling as if she were trapped in a bad dream.

"Do you have an appointment?"

"No. I don't."

"Your name, please?"

"Joanna Clooney."

The woman picked up a phone on the sleekly modern desk and spoke her name. After a moment she hung up and said smoothly, "Won't you come with me, please?" She led Joanna up a staircase to a beautiful, open living space on the second floor.

"Mr. O'Connor will be right with you," the woman said with a small smile and a blatant glimmer of curiosity, before turning to go back downstairs.

Looking around at the sculpted architectural purity of the high ceilings and curving fanlight windows, the spare, impeccable furnishings, Joanna remembered Reid's passion for beautiful spaces. And the passion that he'd once felt for her.

She turned swiftly away from the painful memory to cast a professional eye over the paintings on those wide swaths of wall. Evidently he'd prospered. Only last month she'd gone to view the Christopher Pratt that hung above the fireplace when it came up for auction, and it had commanded a very good price. Obviously Reid could now afford the kind of life he'd always wanted.

By getting rid of her, he could now enjoy that life without being shackled to a wife who came far below his precious work on his list of priorities.

That she had been an encumbrance had been made very plain by his swift, cold-blooded way of handling the divorce. He'd asked her father to act as go-between, sparing him even the necessity of seeing her. All she'd done was sign a few papers and given him his cherished freedom.

After all that, whatever possessed her to think, even for a second, that he'd be interested in helping her now?

2

REID PUT DOWN the phone and stared at it. It felt as if his brain had just exploded.

He'd just heard his assistant's familiar voice telling him that Joanna Clooney was here to see him. And his own automatic reply, "Show her up, Beth." And here he was, still staring at the phone like some stunned fool.

He looked up and saw his face gazing back at him from the dresser mirror. Good, at least he still looked the same. Nobody would guess that he'd just been hit by the proverbial thunderbolt out of the blue.

"You pathetic fool," he sneered at his reflection. "Get a grip."

He turned away from the dresser and walked over to the closet.

"What the hell does she want?" he muttered irritably as he grabbed his suit jacket off the hanger. He paused with a cynical chuckle. "Because you know she wants something from you, and it *isn't* you, pal."

He shrugged into the jacket, feeling better now he'd got some perspective again. She'd already discarded him once, like all the other things she got bored with. Well, for him, once was enough.

Moving back to check the knot of his tie in the dresser mirror, he made a minute adjustment, his hand rock steady. Yeah, everything was just fine. He glanced up to his face. Color looked good, nothing of his inner turmoil showed. With a nod of satisfaction, he smiled at his reflection. He was ready to face the enemy.

Calm and unhurried, he crossed the large bedroom that took up the whole third floor and headed down the stairs, deliberately unclenching his fists as he went.

She was standing by the window with her back to him. And thank heaven for that. He paused at the bottom of the stairs. It took everything he had just to control his suddenly ragged breathing, but there was nothing he could do to stop the painful pounding of his heart against his ribs.

As if sensing his presence, she turned and stiffened. Her cool gaze swept over him and she gave him that aloof look he remembered oh so well. She was her father's daughter, all right.

"Hello, Reid."

He smiled back. "Joanna. What a surprise." *What bullshit!* He'd been cut off at the knees.

"I'm sure you must be *very* surprised." Her lips curved in a smile, but her voice was tense and brittle.

"How do you mean, surprised? Like when you're going along, minding your own business and someone drops an anvil on your head? That kind of a surprise?"

She blinked, startled out of her self-possessed pose and for a moment the years fell away and he was staring into the pair of amber eyes that had smiled up at him with openness and candor.

In the next second the polite mask was back in place. She stood there so cool and superior . . . and so beautiful. Her nut-brown hair was still long and curly, and there was the tiny mole he remembered so well, just a millimeter beyond the tip of her left brow.

Her skin was still smooth and pale. Was it just his imagination, or was it drawn too tightly over her fine-boned face? A thoroughbred, that's what she was. Five years ago he'd never met anyone like her; she'd dazzled him with all that beauty and poise and sophistication.

It had taken a while to discover that it was all a veneer, the private-school manners and exquisite grooming. Inside she was still Daddy's little princess—craving attention, needing to be taken care of. But now that deceptive packaging had become a hard, impenetrable gloss.

At twenty-five, she was no little girl anymore, and even more beautiful than she had been at twenty. Her kind of looks just kept on getting better. He could hardly wait to see her at thirty-five or forty. From a distance, that is. Self-appointed royalty like Joanna Clooney and her kind were bad news for guys like him.

"Well, however *you* may feel, it's good to see you again," she said.

He raised a questioning eyebrow in reply. To his amazement, a flood of pale pink spread over her cheekbones, the only sign that she wasn't perfectly composed.

"How are you doing?" Her soft, husky voice sent a prickle of anxiety over his skin.

"I'm doing well, and you?"

"Just fine." The small smile didn't quite make it to her eyes. Now that he was looking at her more closely he could see that beyond her cool detachment there was something frozen, numb about her.

He didn't like that look, didn't like the feeling creeping over him. She was in trouble all right, and obviously felt he could help. The question was, did he want to? Hell no! Why should he?

"Forget it, Joanna, you're not just fine. You didn't come to see me because you're fine. Now, what's the problem? And please don't waste my time getting to the point." Whatever her trouble was, he didn't want to get involved.

She winced at his uncompromising tone, but he didn't care. The last time he'd seen her had been at her father's funeral eighteen months, twenty-six days and three hours ago. He'd been stupid enough to think that maybe, in spite of their differences, she'd turn to him. He'd quickly discovered his mistake. Paul LaValliere had been at her elbow. One of Joanna's own kind, smooth, wealthy and dancing attendance on her like a well-bred shadow.

"Aren't you even going to ask me to sit?"

Now she was stalling. This wasn't like Joanna. She'd always known what she wanted and how to go about getting it. He had no reason to believe that had changed.

As he took a step toward her she immediately took a step back. *Interesting*.

He stopped, seeing the guarded look that filled her eyes. Whatever her reasons for coming, it was clear that she didn't want to be here. The thought was grimly amusing.

He gave her a wry smile. "Please, won't you sit down?" With elaborate civility, he waved toward the art-deco armchair behind her.

Deliberately, he moved closer, wanting to see her reaction again, but her fresh, light fragrance filled his head, assaulting his senses. He paused, glad when she took a quick step backwards and sank gracefully onto the velvet seat.

"Thanks," she murmured, primly smoothing the silky white skirt of her suit down over her thighs.

He tore his gaze away from the smooth, soft length of her legs and clenched his teeth. The problem was, he liked to watch her; he always had. There was something so intrinsically graceful, so feminine about Joanna it drew him like a magnet.

"Please," she burst out suddenly, her voice tense, "it's very disconcerting having you standing over me."

Too bad. It's disconcerting just having you here. He sat down on the matching sofa and leaned back, stretching his legs out in front of him and crossing them at the ankles. The silence lengthened as he examined his black Italian loafers.

"You've got a very nice place here," she said finally. "You've done well for yourself."

How predictable of her to notice, to assess and pass judgment. Would he be considered good enough for her *now*? He felt the pulse beating erratically beside his mouth and tried hard to suppress it, but he couldn't keep the irritation out of his voice. "Yes, I have. Surprised?"

She gave him a cool, condescending smile. "No, not at all. I'm very happy everything worked out for you."

"Are you?" He smiled, but couldn't keep the old bitterness from surfacing. "And just think, I have you to thank for everything. If you hadn't left me, I probably wouldn't be where I am today." With a careless shrug, he waved a hand around the beautiful room. Today he was a man who knew himself, what he wanted and what he needed. What he didn't need was Joanna Clooney back in his life.

"Look, it was hard enough to come here in the first place. I can understand that you're angry, but—"

"Angry!" He gave a short, humorless laugh. "I'm not angry, I'm grateful. You gave me a way out of the biggest mistake of my life."

He'd just confirmed what she'd known all along, so why did it feel as if something in her had just died? Everything she could think to say sounded unbearably trite. So she said nothing, just allowed her gaze to run compulsively over him.

He was still the handsomest man she'd ever seen. When they were together she'd been used to seeing him in work clothes—jeans and T-shirts thick with sawdust and building-site grime. Now, in a dark navy suit that hung perfectly on his broad shoulders, he radiated the kind of success and power he'd always desired above everything else.

He'd changed in the past three years. This new Reid looked grim and formidably self-possessed. Yet that raw, dangerous, unpredictable streak still burned in him. She could see it, a steely glint buried deep in his eyes. Cold despair spread through her. Why was she even here?

"Now . . . what can I do to help you?"

"It's not about me," she said lifelessly. "It's about my mother."

At last she saw a sharpening in the dispassionate gaze, and she felt a tiny seed of hope.

"What about your mother?" There was a tinge of alarm in his deep voice.

She rushed to allay his obvious fear. "It's not what you think."

"Then what is it?" He looked a little wary, and his voice hardened again.

A defeated sigh escaped her. How could she have thought, even for an instant, that he'd want to help her?

"My mother, she . . . she woke up."

"What did you say?" Suddenly alert, he leaned toward her, a satisfying intensity blazing in his eyes.

The little withered seed of optimism began to take root again. "She woke up a few weeks ago, and she wants to see you."

"My God!" he murmured to himself in disbelief, a slow smile of wonder curving his firm mouth.

He shot to his feet and walked restlessly over to the window, every movement imbued with the potent masculine grace that was his alone, taking her back to the moment she first saw him.

He'd been surveying the half-built art studio that her father had given her as a twentieth-birthday present. He was only five years older, already a junior partner in the construction firm he now owned, and he'd been assigned to supervise the job.

It wasn't just the golden-brown hair and boyish good looks that had caught her attention; the intensity burning in his smoky gray eyes, the power and earthiness he exuded made every other man vanish into insignificance.

The attraction had been instant and explosive. Her father had strongly disapproved of their whirlwind romance, but by the time of their marriage, only three months later, her mother had brought him around. She'd liked Reid, and said he had "character."

"How is she doing?" His voice brought her back from the past. He wasn't looking at her, but stood gazing out across the treetops to the city towers rising in the distance.

"She's doing fine, so far.... She wants to see you."

"Of course! I'll go this afternoon." Now he turned to her and smiled, obviously thinking their meeting was over.

Tension gripped her as she rose to her feet. Turning away, she walked stiffly toward the fireplace and looked up at the serene Pratt seascape without really seeing it. How was she going to continue?

She cleared her throat. "There's something else."

There was a short pause. When he spoke, he sounded calm, but his voice held a note of foreboding. "And what might that be?"

Turning slowly, she met his gaze. His cool gray eyes betrayed no sign as to what he was thinking. But she knew that he was aware of every emotion, every thought, every memory—everything she was feeling. What was the point in trying to hide anything from him? He knew her too well.

"When my mother asked for you, I didn't tell her . . . I couldn't tell her, that we're divorced."

Something quickened in his eyes, but his voice remained quiet and unhurried, almost uncaring. "Why not?"

"I was afraid that the shock might be too much. I had to tell her about Dad, you see. I just couldn't tell her about us too. . . ." Her voice trailed off abruptly at the inscrutable expression on his face.

"So she thinks we're still married!"

"Yes."

Absolute silence fell in the room. Reid turned away to stare out the window again, hands shoved in the pockets of his navy trousers. She was grateful. She didn't think she could have stood the pressure of that invasive scrutiny a second longer.

As the silent moments slid by, he remained like a statue, except for the small angry pulse beating erratically by the corner of his mouth.

A sudden image came into her head unbidden, shocking her, taking her breath away. She remembered pressing her lips against that pulse to soothe him, to dissipate his anger. It had worked. He'd given in to her with a mixture of frustration and desire. That is, back at the very beginning, when she'd been able to entice him away from his work to make love. Love in the afternoon.

It was impossible to believe that she'd ever had that kind of power over this hard, tough-as-nails man.

When he slowly turned to look at her, the implacable determination on his face made the breath leave her lungs in a painful gasp.

"We've got to tell her the truth. We can't lie to her. Not about something like this."

She took quick agitated steps toward him. "Why not?"

"Come on, Joanna, do you need it spelled out?" He shook his head, still very calm. "*No.* She's got to be told the truth."

"I can't." She twisted her cold hands together. "I just can't."

"Why not?"

"It would be too much of a shock. I couldn't risk her health like that." She reached toward him, pleading.

He took her hands, his strong fingers warm on her chilled skin and his voice more gentle. "Joanna, we can't lie to your mother. We have to tell her the truth."

She wrenched away from him, surprised at the violence of her own emotions. She didn't want his gentleness now, didn't want to hear his reasonable tone. "I won't do it! I can't do it."

"Joanna, listen to me—"

"No! I don't expect you to understand, but I can't and won't tell her about us. Not yet." She paused for breath. "You know my mother—this will crush her."

He gave her a long, unreadable look. "So when do you plan on telling her? The longer you leave it, the harder it'll get, you know."

"No," she insisted desperately. "The longer I wait, the stronger she'll get, and maybe then she'll be able to deal with it."

"And what do you propose in the meantime?"

"In the meantime—" she paused to muster her courage "—I would really appreciate it if you could just pretend that we're still married."

For a moment he just stared at her, incredulous. She held her breath.

"Have you lost your mind?" he exploded, his eyes blazing with anger.

She winced. For a moment she wondered if indeed she had lost her mind, but then remembered that frail figure in the hospital and knew that there was no other way.

"It would only have to be for a short while," she rushed on, "just a couple of months, till she's strong enough."

Reid said nothing, but his thunderstruck expression was eloquent.

"Please try to understand," she begged. "I can't afford to take any risks with her health. I don't want to lose my mother again."

"Are you insane?" He was a little calmer now, but just as implacable. "We can't just pretend that we're still married. Do you have any idea what you're asking?"

He hadn't heard a word she'd just said. "Of course I know what I'm asking."

"You're asking me to lie to her. I won't do it. Now we're going to go to that hospital, you and I together, and we're going to see Louise, *together*, and tell her the truth."

"Do you think it's easy for me to lie?" she demanded, full of anger and resentment. He was acting as if this was some selfish whim of hers. "If I knew for certain that she'd be all right with the truth, I'd tell her right now. But I can't be sure of anything and I won't take that risk."

She took a step toward him and then regretted her hasty, unthinking action. With scant inches between them, she could feel the heat of his body, smell the clean fragrance of his soap mixed with that indefinable scent of his that evoked painful, vivid memories.

She took a hasty step back, but he closed the distance between them.

"Contrary to what you think, I do still care about her. I still want to be part of her life and help her in any way I can. But we're going to tell her the truth. We owe her that, don't you think?"

"No, I don't think. Not now. But when the time comes, she'll understand why we had to lie. At any rate, we'll deal with it then."

He shook his head in derisive amazement and she tried to steel herself against his contempt.

"What you're asking is impossible."

"Why?"

"So many reasons, but here's the clincher. I'm engaged to be married." His mouth twisted with grim humor. "And I don't think my bride-to-be would appreciate your arrangement."

"Engaged?" The news took her breath away like a fist in the solar plexus. "But who? How? When?"

"Does any of that matter right now?" His voice barely penetrated her dazed consciousness.

"No, of course not. Congratulations," she managed faintly. *Married? He would belong to someone else?*

"Thanks," he said evenly, his expression sober. "And the same to you, I believe?"

"Yes . . . I wasn't sure if you'd know." She felt like a robot, hardly aware of the words coming out of her mouth as she looked at him, compulsively drinking in every detail of his face, as if this were the last time she'd ever see him.

His wry smile was utterly without humor. "I read the papers from time to time. When the owner of the most successful gallery in the country becomes engaged to a millionaire art collector like Paul LaValliere, it makes the news."

"Yes, of course," she answered automatically, still in a daze. Until this moment she'd never realized that she still regarded Reid as belonging to her, in spite of the divorce.

"What does your fiancé think about all this? Surely he's not happy about this harebrained idea of yours."

"He understands." Paul always understood.

"Then he's a bloody fool," he muttered, turning away from her to frown out the window.

"He's not a fool." A wave of despondency threatened to overtake her. She had to rally herself. "He happens to be a very smart man and I value his opinion."

"He's also a wealthy guy with a lot of spare time to lavish on you. Sounds tailor-made."

He turned his head and his slow, knowing gaze ran over her, lingering on the V of her white silk suit jacket. There was nothing provocative about the cut, but all at once she felt naked. Then he grinned. "Good in bed, is he?"

A rush of heat made her cheeks burn. "That's none of your business!"

He chuckled, but she could hear the thread of derision. He was laughing at her and it hurt.

Did he remember how good *they* had been together? Did he remember the shape and feel of her body, as she remembered his? How she'd trembled with feverish desire in his arms? She licked her suddenly dry lips.

He became grim. "We've strayed from the point. We have to tell your mother the truth. I'll come to the hospital with you."

All hope that he might help her had died the moment Reid told her he was going to marry someone else. She said quickly, "No. No, that won't be necessary. I'll tell her myself tomorrow morning. I'm sorry I took up so much of your time. Goodbye."

Before he had time to say anything, she turned and moved toward the stairs.

When she reached the ground floor, Joanna rushed past the woman seated at the desk, and out the front door.

She'd failed in her mission. But that wasn't the only reason that her eyes burned with tears and it felt like a heavy weight had taken up permanent residence in her heart.

Reid stood at the window and watched Joanna emerge from the house and walk quickly to the white Porsche parked out front. She slid into the driver's seat, slammed the door and drove away.

He took a deep breath, closed his eyes and leaned his forehead against the cool glass for a moment, willing the tension to dissipate. But every muscle clenched tighter until he thought that something inside him would snap.

He turned to look around. This place would never be the same again. Already traces of her filled the room, painful reminders. The dented chair cushion where she'd sat, the faint lingering fragrance of her delicate perfume. *Damn!* She permeated the very air around him.

He closed his eyes to block out the image of her here, in this room, and recalled every detail. She was still spoiled and used to getting her way, but she seemed harder now, more ruthless. As if she'd walk over anybody to get what she wanted.

But in some ways it was only to be expected. What she'd gone through in the past three years was enough to make anyone grow up in a hurry, even Joanna.

But God, she was still so beautiful and so sexy. Despite everything, he'd only had to look at her to want her, to ache to touch her, as he'd once had the right to. It was not surprising that he'd still respond to her that way. After all, sex had been the basis of the attraction, that wild passion he'd thought was love. But real love wasn't selfish and destructive. If they'd really loved each other, nothing could have split them up.

But their marriage had been doomed for another reason: his naive failure to realize that she was out of his league. Five years ago he'd stupidly felt proud that a regular guy like him had captured the heart of a girl who had her pick of far more eligible men.

He sighed and pressed a hand to his lids, trying to block out the tormenting images that crowded his mind. He could never trust her, and he could never let her close enough to mess him up again.

Seeing Joanna today had reminded him how disastrous marriage could be with the wrong person. It had made one thing crystal-clear. He couldn't marry anyone else. Not yet. Maybe not ever.

3

JOANNA PULLED INTO the parking lot of the private hospital and switched off the engine, but instead of getting out of the car she sat staring through the windshield at the glossy, wet leaves of the lilac bushes bordering the lot.

Through the long, dark hours of the night she'd lain awake, listening to the splash of the spring rain on her bedroom window and trying to figure out how on earth she was going to tell her mother the truth.

Reluctantly she opened the car door and stepped out, steeling herself to go in and get it over and done with as quickly as possible. As she began walking toward the front doors she noticed a figure emerging from a dark green Jaguar parked in the circular drive.

Joanna stopped dead in her tracks. Her heart seemed to cease beating for a moment, then lurched into a slow, painful throb.

Reid walked toward her through the warm drifts of mist, as insubstantial as a ghost, until she saw his eyes, narrow and glittering and fixed on her with unrelenting purpose.

She couldn't meet those eyes, instead she allowed her gaze to slide down over the length of his body. Big mistake.

His butter-soft tan leather jacket hung open, over an oxford-cloth shirt that hugged the contours of his chest and was unbuttoned at the throat, revealing a golden triangle of skin. How well she remembered being wrapped in his arms, her body molded to his, her lips nuzzling that very spot.

She dropped her gaze, afraid he'd see the memory in her eyes, but that only made it worse. She stared at his flat stomach, the brown leather belt of the twill pants riding lean hips. He looked hard as granite and sinfully sexy.

A surge of heat rushed up through her body, to flame into her cheeks. With a tiny gasp of embarrassment she focused her gaze on his face once again, only to find the same cruelly acute scrutiny holding her like an invisible hand.

Swallowing hard, she lifted her chin in a bid for composure as he came closer. How could she be reacting to him so intensely at a time like this?

He stopped a couple of feet away and shoved his hands into his jacket pockets with that imperturbable calm that she found so unsettling.

Just being near him was impossible. Inside her, every nerve quivered with tension. No matter how hard she tried to quell the feeling, there was something in her that responded to him, against her will, against her reason. It made her feel helpless and she recoiled from that kind of weakness.

"I can do this on my own, you know," she said.

"I'm sure you can." His voice was cool and steady. "I just think it would be better to do it together."

"But this doesn't concern you."

He said nothing, only raised an eyebrow. The dull heat surged back into her face. He wasn't even going to dignify that stupid statement with a reply. Why had she ever brought him into this?

"Look," she said hurriedly, "you have your own life, your own problems. Go back to them and let me handle mine."

"I can't do that," he insisted.

"Why not?" Desperation edged her voice.

"I feel responsible for Louise . . . for you."

Her heart gave a small breathless leap before she quickly reminded herself that this was typical of his exaggerated sense of duty. It didn't really mean anything.

"You don't need to feel responsible for me. I can take care of myself."

"My, how things have changed."

His small, condescending smile made her grit her teeth and count to ten. She refused to let his sarcasm provoke her into defending herself.

He thought her parents had spoiled her, had raised a daughter incapable of doing anything worthwhile. True, she had grown up with every advantage, but that didn't make her a useless person. And in the past three years she'd had to find out what she was made of. But she didn't need his approval. Let him think what he wanted of her.

"I think we're getting away from the point. I don't *need* you here. I can do this on my own."

"I'm not doing this for you," he said quietly, "I'm doing this for Louise. I think it would be easier on her to know I'm still around and that I still care about what happens to her."

"And what I want doesn't count?"

"That's right." His words were soft and unequivocal.

She turned on her heel and headed for the main entrance. Reid fell into step at her side. As they reached the door he swiftly opened it for her.

Joanna strode quickly for the stairs, keeping her resentful gaze turned away from him, but acutely conscious of his lean, vital figure right beside her. No matter how fast she walked, it was impossible to distance herself from the way he affected her. Getting too close to that white-hot intensity made her afraid she'd burn up.

He was close behind her when she slowly began to open the door at the end of the hall. Her mother was sitting reading in a chair by the open window.

Joanna heard Reid's sudden intake of breath and felt his long fingers close over hers to prevent the door opening fully. A slow warm tide of sensation spread up her arm. But he didn't see her betraying reaction; his worried gaze was fixed on her mother, who was not yet aware of their presence.

"She looks so small, so fragile," he murmured and she could see the concern tugging down the corners of his mouth.

Then her mother looked up, and all thoughts of her own feelings fled when she saw the smile of pure gladness lighting her mother's face.

"Reid!" Laying the book down on a small table, she held out her thin arms to him.

"Louise." He strode across the room, sank down on one knee beside her chair and wrapped her in a tender hug that almost swallowed up the frail body. "It's so good to see you."

The thickness in his voice brought tears to Joanna's eyes. The last of her resentment for his high-handedness dissipated right there.

Her mother kissed his cheek and his eyes closed, an expression of desperate thankfulness on his face. There was something touching and special about the bond between them.

Joanna turned away from this private moment, overwhelmed by a piercing, bittersweet gladness. He still loved her mother. He just didn't love *her*.

She turned back to see him slowly pulling away and getting to his feet, but he still kept a tight hold on the thin hands.

"How are you feeling?"

"I've been in a coma for three years, what do you think?" The spirited reply was a little shaky. "I'm glad to be feeling anything at all."

He chuckled, then turned and glanced at Joanna, amusement gleaming in his eyes. "She's back."

"With a vengeance," Joanna murmured, a rueful smile curving her mouth.

Then suddenly the warmth died in his expression, leaving it dark and guarded. He turned back to her mother. "It's good to see you haven't lost your sense of humor, but really, how *do* you feel?"

"Now that we're all together again, wonderful." Beaming up at him, she tugged on the long, slender fingers entwined with hers. "Now sit, you're giving me a crick in my neck."

With another one of those lopsided smiles that made Joanna's heart catch in her throat, he took the other chair. Her mother looked so happy, and so vulnerable. How was she going to tell her the truth?

"Was your business trip successful?"

"Yes...." He hesitated, glancing quickly at Joanna, his eyes asking for some clue as to what she might have told her. "Yes, very successful."

"Where did you go?"

"Umm...Vancouver Island." Exasperation narrowed his eyes. If looks could kill...

"Don't you take your wife with you when you go on these trips?"

Joanna groaned inwardly. Just like her irrepressible parent to make matters worse.

Reid turned and fixed her with a look that could peel paint. Burning heat flooded her cheeks.

"My wife," he began with deliberate irony, "is usually too busy with her own life to accompany me."

"Joanna, that's no way to treat your husband. Especially one who loves you as much as Reid does."

The corner of his long, straight mouth twitched with amusement at her chiding tone.

Joanna shot him a ferocious look, and grappled with the urge to throw something at him, but he only responded with a taunting smile.

"I have a business to run, Mom." Her voice was rigid with resentment. "I don't have time to go gallivanting to the west coast with him."

Her mother's gaze sharpened as it darted back and forth between them, and then a worried look deepened the green of her eyes. "I've been a strain on you two, haven't I?"

"No! Of course not!" they both said in unison, and Joanna felt alarmed and guilty at how she'd let her personal feelings supersede her mother's needs.

"Not in the way you think, Louise." Reid sounded so calm and reasonable, but his composure stretched her nerves even tighter. "Everything is—"

"Mom—" Joanna couldn't stand this contest of who was going to crack first for another second, "—Reid and I have something we want to talk to you about."

Involuntarily her gaze darted to Reid. He sat still and waiting, but she could see that small pulse beating at the corner of his mouth. "Reid and I . . ." she began again hesitantly, her heart speeding up. She just couldn't bring herself to say the words. "We . . ."

"What Joanna's trying to say is that we want to take you home as soon as possible," he cut in smoothly, calm and decisive.

Joanna gaped at him in astonishment. What was he doing? *Why* was he doing this?

"Oh, I'd like that very much." Her mother's happy voice reached her dimly through the shock. "But I don't want to be a burden on you kids."

"Don't be silly, you're not a burden." He sounded so glib, so reassuring that he almost had *her* convinced everything was perfectly normal between them. Whatever he was feeling was carefully hidden behind that urbane exterior. "Don't you think you've been in this place long enough?"

"I'll say!"

The sheer joy and relief in the shaky voice finally penetrated Joanna's shock. She looked down and saw the adoration on her mother's face as she gazed at Reid and a shooting pain pierced her heart. The truth was going to hurt her so much.

"I'll speak to Dr. Malcho before I leave."

"I'll start packing." Her mother chuckled: a young, carefree sound.

"Now hold on." Joanna felt a tinge of alarm mixed with annoyance. Things were suddenly moving at a very quick pace, thanks to Reid. "I'm sure Dr. Malcho would have said something already if she felt you were fit enough to leave."

"There's no harm in asking, Joanna." He sounded mild and reasonable. He even smiled.

"No harm at all," her mother added with a new lightness in her voice.

She had to get him out of here before he said anything more!

She stood up quickly. "You're right, there's no harm in asking." She smiled at her mother, looking so happy, so fragile, with a calm she certainly didn't feel.

Reid rose too, took the thin fingers in his large, capable hand and raised them to his lips, a warm smile crinkling the corners of his eyes as he pressed a kiss on her fingertips. "We'll be back tomorrow."

"You're a good boy. I feel better now that you're here to take care of us."

Joanna stiffened with resentment. Hadn't she been doing just fine all this time without his help?

He straightened and turned to face her and her resentment increased. Why *was* he helping? Now that he had only her for an audience, his feelings were quite painfully obvious. Anger simmered in his eyes. He obviously still didn't want to do it. So why had he made that ridiculous offer?

With a supreme effort, she swallowed her bitterness and leaned over to give her mother a kiss. She was in no position to look a gift horse in the mouth. "'Bye, I'll see you tomorrow."

The warm, shockingly familiar touch of Reid's hand on her waist made her stiffen. Sudden, red-hot need exploded through her, a violent longing to be *really* touched by him.

She straightened and tried to draw away, but he put his arm around her shoulder, then bent to plant a kiss on her mother's thin cheek.

"Have a good day and don't tire yourself out," he ordered gently as he straightened and his hand slid back down to Joanna's waist. How could he not feel her trembling?

"I will, now." With a smile of contentment, the tired gaze went from one to the other of them, and Joanna noticed a new look in her eyes, a glimmer of strength and purpose. She couldn't deny that Reid had brought about this miraculous change.

Forcing her numb facial muscles to respond, she smiled back, in what she prayed was a natural way, then walked stiffly out of the room. All the while Reid's warm, firm hand rested on the small of her back, the little finger splayed over the point where the curve of her buttocks began.

As soon as the door closed behind him she lunged away from the light touch that burned into her flesh like a searing brand. She turned to face him, her hands clasped tightly behind her back against the very spot where his fingers had rested.

"What's the matter?"

"How can you ask? I thought you said you didn't want to lie to her."

The corners of his wide mouth curved in a faint, derisive smile. "I thought so, too."

"So what changed your mind?" She tried to suppress the small germ of hope that she still mattered to him in some way.

"I don't know." He shrugged and gave her a wry look. "I guess some things never change. Whenever I'm around you, my judgment gets shot to hell."

"Oh sure, blame me." It was impossible not to feel a little bitter at entertaining the thought, even for a second, that he might still care for her.

His mouth compressed with impatience. "Don't be so touchy. You know the reason as well as I do." He shook his head, looking resigned and disgusted with himself as he said gruffly, "I just couldn't do it. I couldn't hurt her like that. You were right, she's not ready to hear that particular news yet." She could see how much it galled him to admit she was right. "Look, we need to go somewhere and talk."

"About what?"

"About getting your mother out of this place to come and live with us."

"Come and—!" She bit back the shocked exclamation and lowered her voice, moving farther down the corridor, away from her mother's room. "Come and live with us! You can't be serious."

"Of course I'm serious. There's no reason for her to be in this place any longer. We'd have to hire a nurse—"

"Wait a minute." Joanna shook her head in disbelief. "You're forgetting something. *We* don't have a place."

"Then *we* are going to have to get one," he explained evenly.

"What!" She felt as if someone had just pulled the ground out from under her.

"Haven't you given this any thought?" Annoyance hardened his voice. "What did you think telling your mother we're still married would mean? Didn't you realize that we'd have to live as if we were married?"

"I didn't have time to realize anything." She felt panic-stricken. "But that's beside the point. You could have at least discussed it with me first instead of just telling her she was going to come home and live with us."

"What else could I tell her? She'd expect us to be living together. And I can't see any other way around it if we're going to carry this off."

"Well, I can." Desperation gave conviction to her words. There was no way she'd carry this pretense as far as living with him. The very thought sent a violent tremor of fear through her.

"And what might that be?"

"Simple. *I* take her home. It is her home, after all, and she'll just assume that I've moved in to be with her for a while and, obviously, that you don't mind."

"But I would mind and she knows it. I would never let you go away for so long—it could be months. Naturally I'd go with you. She'd expect it."

She felt desperate, caught in a trap of her own making. Why did his objections have to make so much sense? There had to be a way to make her plan work, but right now not one single solution occurred to her.

"We could come up with at least a dozen reasons why it would be better for you to stay home."

"All of which she'd override. You know she would. As it is, she's worried enough about coming between us."

Joanna squirmed, turned away from him and wrapped her arms tightly across her waist as the full horror of the situation dawned on her.

What a fool she had been, what a blind fool! How could she not have thought ahead to the consequences of the deception? And to make things worse, Reid had anticipated everything. He'd been using his head.

Just because she'd been too overwrought to think clearly was no excuse for not thinking at all.

"Maybe, if you visited a lot . . ." she began with a faint spark of hope, turning back to face him. He briefly shook his head. Aware of how impossibly lame the idea sounded, her voice weakened. "Maybe she wouldn't notice that you're not actually living there."

"Do you really think so? Come on, Joanna, there's no other way. And after all, it was your idea in the first place."

She couldn't argue with that, but she had to try. "But not like this. I never meant like this."

"I'm afraid *this* is the only way."

JOANNA COULD SEE the Jag in her rearview mirror as Reid followed her through the shady tree-lined streets to the wooded estate perched on rugged clay bluffs overlooking Lake Ontario.

She drove through the open iron gates and followed the winding drive past the statues and marble pillars that her parents had collected over the years.

The rambling stone house came into view through the trees, and somehow just seeing it gave her a feeling of safety, of permanence. The one place that was her refuge. The house where she'd grown up, the house to which she'd retreated after their marriage blew up in her face.

Here she'd found a home again, and for the first time in her life the feeling of being needed. Her father had been lost after her mother's accident, and he'd increasingly depended on her to run his life. Before long she was running his gallery too, and finding out at last what she was capable of.

Reid pulled his car up behind hers, then joined her at the front door. He stood beside her, close enough that she could feel his warmth. Her hand shook a little as she pulled out her key and fitted it in the lock.

"A Clooney opening a door for herself?" His sarcasm made her grit her teeth. "Where's Halton?"

"It's his day off," she said stiffly.

"For a moment I thought you'd dispensed with the services of a butler and joined the real world. Stupid of me."

His contempt hurt, but she pushed the pain aside. This was no time to dwell on wounded feelings. She had a *real* problem on her hands. She led him inside and down a hallway to the large, well-appointed kitchen, the quiet house filled with a heavy silence that sharpened her awareness of the intensity he radiated.

While the coffee dripped she busied herself putting out the mugs, cream and sugar on the kitchen table. Reid had settled into one of the press-back pine chairs and sat silently watching her. His quiet, unwavering gaze followed her movements, as disturbing and tangible a sensation as that warm hand at the base of her spine.

Finally she brought the steaming pot to the table and his continuing silence nettled her into speech. "What about your fiancée? Won't she mind?"

"That doesn't need to concern you," he said offhandedly.

"Now where have I heard that before?" She couldn't keep the sarcasm from her voice as she poured the coffee. "You have a lot of nerve! You take over my affairs without so much as a by-your-leave, but I'm not allowed to even be curious about yours."

"You asked for my help—"

"I'm tired of being reminded about that," she snapped tersely, then deliberately quelled her frustration. This wasn't getting them anywhere.

She sat down and faced him across the table, making a tent of her fingers. "Okay. I asked for your help and I appreciate it. But you had no right to tell my mother you were going to arrange for her release. From now on, kindly leave the decision-making to me."

"Gladly." He nodded his head with a brief glimmer of mockery. The familiar mask of boredom came down over his face. She remembered that look from the old days. How she'd always hated it.

Back then it had made her feel foolish and childish, and even now it had exactly the same effect. Except that then he might have had good reason for such a look. When she'd first met Reid, she'd been immature for her age and plagued with terminal self-doubt. But not any longer.

She was a woman now and sure enough of herself to know that her resentment was valid.

"Now, can we discuss the real problem?" he said.

"Which is?"

"If the object of this whole charade is to spare your mother worry, then we'd better be more convincing than we were today. Don't you think it'll bother her when she begins to notice that we hold each other in contempt?"

"I don't hold you in contempt!" Her head swam a little and she felt sick. So that was the way he felt about her.

His brow lifted sceptically. "You can't even stand being touched by me."

What could she say? It was useless to deny it, he'd felt her response. She should be glad that he hadn't guessed the real reason.

His eyes narrowed so that she couldn't read their expression, but the infinitesimal curl of his upper lip spoke volumes.

A huge lump settled in her throat, and she willed back the hot tears gathering behind her eyes. She could take anything except his contempt.

But when he spoke again his voice was mild, almost neutral. "Like it or not, we're going to have to live together in the same house and do everything a happily married couple would do."

"Forget it!" The words exploded out of her as a vivid, tantalizing image filled her head, of being wrapped in his arms, naked limbs entwined, as they made love all through one long, quiet afternoon in this very house, in her own room upstairs, while her parents were away.

He'd had the power to make her body come alive, the power to make her forget everything except making love with him.

A rush of heat flooded through every vein, and her mouth went dry. Oh yes, that part of their relationship had always been very good for them. Tempestuous, in fact. Reid had been an insatiable, passionate lover.

"I meant, everything a husband and wife would do in front of other people." The smile became mocking.

"Oh." Her gaze dropped to the steaming mug in front of her. The heat seared her cheeks and she felt stupid for jumping to such a conclusion. It was disturbing how easily she could fall prey to that insidious allure he still held for her.

"Including kissing."

Her startled gaze flew to his face and found him watching her impassively.

"I think we should have a dress rehearsal before the performance."

"We don't need to ... to rehearse that! We don't need to kiss each other at all." The very thought filled her with cold panic.

"If you don't want your mother to have any worries about our relationship, she'll expect it. We used to be at each other all the time."

His distaste for their long-ago passion showed her clearly that it wasn't a memory he wanted to dwell on. The realization brought a new dimension of pain.

"That was at the beginning," she said sharply. "No one expects people who've been married for five years to act like newlyweds." With doomed certainty, she knew now that the more time she spent with him, the deeper that pain would go.

"Nevertheless, if we want to be convincing we have to play our parts. I don't like this any more than you, but remember—"

"Yes, I know. It was my idea in the first place," she said bitterly.

It made him smile. But this time she saw genuine amusement in his face, and even a tinge of pity. She paused, arrested by the transformation. He looked softer, less intimidating, more like the man she had once fallen in love with.

"Okay, I can see your point," she finally conceded.

After all, he *was* right. Her mother would expect some signs of affection between them. And it might be easier to get the first time over and done with when there weren't any witnesses to her discomfort. But not that much easier.

He rose from the table, leaving his coffee untouched, and she realized that he meant to kiss her right now.

She struggled to her feet, trying to appear cool and unconcerned. "As long as we don't have to do this too often—"

"Amen to that," he cut in fervently.

The sudden shaft of painful indignation was totally groundless, but it made her voice sharp. "And at least we won't have to share the same bedroom."

"Oh, yes we will."

His quiet, determined words made her gasp. "What!"

"If I can put up with the inconvenience, so can you."

"We'll have twin beds."

"We'll have nothing of the sort. Twin beds went out with Doris Day."

"You can't possibly expect me to—" she licked her suddenly dry lips and swallowed hard "—to sleep with you."

"I certainly do. But I don't expect you to have sex with me, if that's what's worrying you."

Her breath rushed out in relief, then she saw his mouth quiver as he stepped away from the table. He found it amusing to watch her squirm.

"Now, if you don't mind, let's get this business over and done with. I've got a lot of work ahead of me today."

"You're right. I've got a lot of work to do too." Her voice sounded brittle as she raised her chin with bravado. But walking around the table toward him, she felt like Joan of Arc approaching the stake.

He watched her come closer without a flicker of emotion in his eyes. That didn't fool her for a moment. He was enjoying himself at her expense.

Squaring her shoulders, she tilted her chin even higher. Inside she might be trembling like jelly, but she prided herself that no one, not even Reid, would be able to tell.

A foot away from him she stopped, irresolute. What if she gave herself away by responding? No, she *mustn't*. She must act as if this kiss didn't mean anything.

But as she stood there dithering he reached out and wrapped his fingers around her arms, and brought her gently toward him. Only inches away now, he paused and looked down into her eyes. She stared back, mesmerized.

His impassivity melted away and the gray eyes darkened and filled with a brooding, disturbed look. And something else deep down, a flicker of hunger that caused the desire to stir and blossom painfully in Joanna's body. In vain, she tried to keep it in check.

Suddenly he lifted his head and put her away from him. The dark desire had vanished from his face, replaced by a lazy, mocking smile.

"To tell you the truth, I'm not sure I'm ready for such a momentous event quite yet," he said lightly. "I need a little time to psych myself up for it."

"Yes, me too." Trying for the same offhand tone, she could only manage a painful croak.

"I'd better be going. I'll call you later and we'll discuss arrangements further." He was still smiling, but there was something forced, even grim about it. Then he turned and walked out through the kitchen doorway.

Still stunned, Joanna watched him go. She heard the front door shut, and suddenly began to tremble. His touch had unlocked something inside her, had roused emotions that came soaring painfully to the surface, feelings she had determinedly suppressed.

If it weren't for her mother, she'd turn and run from him, as far and as quickly as possible. But she couldn't run away from this.

And now for the next few months she'd have to see Reid every day, sleep beside him at night. She would have to pretend that she desired him, and hide the fact that it was true. Hide it from a man who had always been able to read her like a book. It was almost like divine retribution for the lie she'd involved him in.

How long would it take for him to find out that she still wanted him? And how would she protect herself from him when he did?

4

REID WALKED to his car, got in and automatically put the key in the ignition. But instead of starting the engine, he stared blindly through the windshield. Why was he doing this? He was only setting himself up for trouble. As sure as night followed day, it would all explode in his face again, and he'd have no one to blame but himself.

He should walk away. Hell, he should run! His mouth twisted with derision as he turned the key and the engine purred to life. Too late now, he was committed.

You're a fool, a real sucker. "Yeah, and a whole lot more besides," he muttered under his breath.

But he had no choice. Louise was too frail to handle any more bad news. He clenched his jaw with determination. After all that woman had done for him, the least he could do was put up with her daughter for a while.

As for how to do that, the solution was simple—he just had to learn not to *feel* anything.

"Yeah, right."

With a cynical chuckle, he put the car in gear and headed for the gate. He kept his eyes fixed on the tree-shaded drive ahead, refusing to look back at the imposing gray stone house receding in the rearview mirror.

The extensive grounds spread out on either side. Through the trees he could see the marble columns and fragments of beautifully sculpted stone the Clooneys had collected. Any one of those pieces would have cost more than it took to support an ordinary family for a year.

It just proved how out of touch people like that were from the world he grew up in. The real world.

That house behind him was a symbol of Joanna's world: a fortress surrounded by walls as impenetrable as they were invisible, walls of snobbery and elitism, designed to keep out the wrong kind of people. It was a world where he didn't belong and never would, no matter how much money he made. He'd dared to think he could just walk in and be part of the club, simply by loving Joanna. Back then, he'd desperately wanted to be accepted. Now he wouldn't join if somebody paid him.

Once, she had been everything to him, the reason he'd pushed so hard for success. Now, all he wanted was to become completely immune to her.

"I DON'T KNOW, dear." The angular, expensively dressed woman stood back a little farther and frowned at the large canvas on the gallery wall. She glanced at her husband, busy murmuring rapidly into his cellular phone, and sighed. "I have a feeling that's not *quite* the shade of blue in the pool-house sofa."

Joanna smothered a groan. Fortunately, the artist was standing on the other side of the gallery. That was just the sort of remark guaranteed to provoke his withering contempt, thereby destroying any chance of a sale.

Tall and gaunt, clad in a black leather jacket and ancient jeans, Alexei could be brooding at the best of times, but right now he looked positively ferocious as he listened to a young stockbroker in a mauve suit telling him what his own paintings were all about.

"You know, Frank, I'm sure that sofa isn't *quite* so turquoise," the woman insisted. Her husband gave the exquisitely detailed canvas one cursory glance and shrugged, then put the phone back to his ear.

Not that she could blame Alexei for being disenchanted with the business of selling art. People like this, with too much money and no real appreciation, made it all too easy to become cynical.

"Frank! You're not listening to me."

Joanna counted slowly to ten, trying to stifle her edginess. What was the matter with her? It wasn't as if she had no experience dealing with clients like this. In her business they were only too common.

Besides, the opening was running perfectly. Her newly renovated gallery made an artfully lit, serene setting for Alexei's wonderful paintings. The invitation-only capacity crowd, well-supplied with wine and hors d'oeuvres by the caterer's expert staff, appeared to be having a good time. She could tell by the buzz of admiration, the subtle hints dropped by the newspaper art critic and the avid interest of her well-heeled clients, that tonight was an unqualified success.

One of the largest canvases was already sold, and if the artist didn't manage to alienate everyone, he'd be the next big thing in the art world. She should be elated and relishing this crowning moment after months of hard work, but somehow something was missing.

Feeling vaguely anxious, she turned and absently searched the crowd. Catching sight of a figure at the door, she froze, every instinct alert and aware. *Reid!*

He stood there slowly scanning the crowded gallery, with a faint, contemptuous curl to his lip.

Unshaven and casually dressed, he effortlessly dominated this room filled with the designer-clad elite. A faint shiver became a surge of excitement and unease rippling through her veins, an awareness of his animal grace and sheer earthy magnetism.

He was undeniably beautiful to look at, but so, so dangerous. How could she forget, even for a second, that he'd broken her heart? She wasn't a kid anymore, confusing sexual attraction with feelings that could form the basis of a solid relationship. Squaring her shoulders, she fought down the involuntary response. She wasn't going to get her heart broken again.

Then his searching gaze found her through the crowd, near the back of the long room. The gray eyes drilled into hers with an intensity that froze her to the spot. His expression was impassive, but she knew what he was thinking. She could see it in the tightening of his jaw, the bored glaze in his eyes. She knew very well that he considered the art world to be a collection of superficial poseurs. Including her, presumably.

"Oh, I don't know," the woman's grating voice met Joanna's ears again. "I *do* like it. But that blue . . ."

"Yeah, honey, you could be right."

Vaguely, Joanna registered the husband's distracted reply, but Reid held her captive. In spite of his obvious scorn, in spite of her determination to guard her heart, all her senses leapt. He was here!

Without conscious thought, she moved toward him, but at that moment he turned on his heel and walked out.

Acute disappointment filled her. The gray pall that had lifted momentarily when he'd walked in, descended again.

She knew why he'd come, and it wasn't because he *wanted* to see her. It was because she'd been avoiding him for the past three days. Ever since that moment in his arms, when his mouth had been only inches away from hers, and she'd realized how desperately she wanted him to kiss her.

But he hadn't kissed her. He'd just left her frustrated, and terrified to go anywhere near him. And after tonight, after that spurt of excitement at the sight of him, she knew she had good reason to be afraid.

The whole situation was like getting caught in quicksand, and feeling a perverse thrill at being sucked inexorably into the treacherous depths. If that wasn't absurd, then she didn't know what was.

A hand closed around her arm. She turned blindly to find Paul smiling down at her, a hint of concern in his dark brown eyes as he examined her face. His elegant, patrician features seemed suddenly unfamiliar.

She blinked in the effort to collect her scattered senses. She'd forgotten about the show, forgotten the couple beside her dithering about the painting, forgotten everything except Reid.

"Come with me," Paul murmured, taking her hand and leading her through the crowd toward the back of the gallery. He opened the door of her office, gently pushed her through and followed, shutting the door behind them.

He picked up two glasses of champagne that sat amongst the litter of papers on her desk, and handed one to her. She took the glass and sipped the wine automatically, not even tasting it.

"Are you all right, Joanna?" A slight frown creased his brow. "You look pale, tense."

That had to be the understatement of the century. She wasn't just tense, she felt as if she were going to explode with anxiety. Overnight, life had become very, very complicated.

"It's nothing. I'm just a little tired." Distractedly, she took another sip of wine. She had to pull herself together. Somehow, she still had to get through the rest of the evening.

"It's no wonder, you've been working around the clock the last few weeks." His deep voice with its slight French accent sounded calm and understanding, but the worried frown remained. "I've hardly seen you at all."

"I'm sorry, I guess I've been—"

"Inaccessible," he finished with a rueful smile. "I feel you've been avoiding me."

A stab of guilt made it difficult for her to meet his uncertain, searching look.

"I'm sorry, Paul. I've been so busy...." Her voice trailed off. Glib excuses wouldn't do and he didn't deserve them, but the truth was, she didn't know what to say.

Between the demands of the gallery and visiting her mother the past few weeks had been crazy. But he was right. She *had* been avoiding him, and she hadn't slept with him since the afternoon Reid had come to her house.

She had told herself that exhaustion and worry had temporarily suppressed her libido. And Paul hadn't pressured her. But she couldn't excuse herself so easily. Around Reid, she was only too easily aroused, and her guilt was unbearable. As if she'd been unfaithful to Paul. And in truth, she had been unfaithful, in her heart.

"I'm sorry," she mumbled, feeling miserable. Those words were so inadequate.

He put down his glass, then took hers and set it on the desk. Taking her in his arms, he pulled her close. She tensed instinctively and had to force herself to relax.

Paul leaned his forehead against hers with a sigh. "No, *I'm* sorry," he said softly, "for being such a selfish monster, for thinking only about my own needs when you have so much on your plate right now. Forgive me?"

"Don't be silly. There's nothing to forgive."

Now she felt more uncomfortable and confused than ever. And even more guilty. She turned away a little and Paul closed his arms around her from behind, resting his chin on the top of her head.

"I should be the one asking your forgiveness," she said awkwardly. "I have been distracted lately. . . ."

"Is it any wonder! I think, all things considered, you've been coping very well. I'm proud of you, Joanna."

"I don't feel very proud of myself. I've made a terrible mess of everything lately. This crazy scheme..." She felt a surge of panic. "Oh, Paul, I must have been insane. It will never work...."

"Now, now, calm down." His voice was low and soothing. "I know this has not been easy for you and it's only just begun, but I want you to know that I'm behind you all the way, no matter what you have to do." He tightened his arms around her and nuzzled her temple.

"I really don't deserve you." Paul's support only made her feel worse, not better.

He'd been so good to her at a time when she really needed a friend. He was attentive, intuitive, sensitive— all the things she needed and wanted from a relationship. Finally, she had achieved a measure of contentment in her life.

Then with one phone call, everything had changed. It had brought the unutterable blessing of having her mother back. But it also brought Reid back into her life, to make her aware that she was only half-alive without even realizing it.

When he was near, that knife-edge awareness, both painful and exquisite, held her in its grip. At those moments it seemed as though everything came brightly, sharply into focus.

Everything except Paul. His image had become cloudy and vague, and she couldn't bear that to happen.

"You've been wonderful about this whole thing with Reid." She'd discussed every aspect of the mock marriage with Paul, in a deliberate effort to dispel any hint of intimacy implicit in the situation. "I don't know anyone else who'd be so understanding."

"Don't get me wrong, I am a little jealous. I'm only human." There was a shade of wry wistfulness in his deep voice. "But I keep reminding myself that you left him, that it didn't work between you. And now you want me. I trust you, Joanna." He turned her around and took her chin gently in his hand as he looked deeply, earnestly into her eyes.

She didn't deserve this man, she didn't deserve his trust. If only she could unburden herself to Paul, confess that she was still sexually attracted to her ex-husband. Could she defuse the danger by just bringing it out into the open?

But that would be needlessly cruel. Reid's allure was that of forbidden fruit, and she wouldn't ruin her relationship with Paul over something so poisonous. How could she confess the attraction, then leave him to stew about it while she and Reid carried out this pretense? She couldn't do that to Paul. She had no intention of acting on the feelings Reid aroused in her. In fact, she planned to fight them with everything she had.

Taking a deep breath, she planted a smile on her lips and looked up into his handsome face. "I've played hooky long enough, I think I'd better get back out there. But thanks for the little break."

"Someone has to look out for you. I'm glad it's me."

He lowered his head and kissed her, his lips warm and gentle, and she made an effort to return his kiss. Maybe she was just tired, maybe it was the guilt over her response to Reid that made her so unresponsive to Paul. These feelings would pass. In the meantime, she wouldn't do anything to hurt him.

She felt relieved when he drew away, turned her around and gave her a little push in the direction of the door.

JOANNA REACHED FOR the switch by her office door and flicked off the main lights, leaving only subdued pools of illumination along the front window and above each painting.

Finally the evening was over. Alexei had gone off complaining about rich, tasteless philistines, but she knew he was secretly pleased that five of those philistines had bought his paintings already. The caterers had packed up and departed, leaving everything spotless. Nothing else remained to be done and now she suddenly felt drained.

"Joanna, you're exhausted." Paul emerged from the office, still looking fresh and immaculate in his beautifully tailored navy suit. "Let me drive you home?"

She smiled gratefully, but shook her head. "Thanks, but no. It would just mean I'd have to take a cab back tomorrow morning."

He put a hand on her upper arm with a gentle caress. "Then at least let me follow, to make sure you get there safely."

The plate glass front door swung open. She looked up and felt her heart jump painfully against her ribs. Reid paused in the doorway, his expression closed, his face half in shadow.

Paul took a step forward. "I'm sorry, the gallery is closed."

An infinitesimal quirk of derision tightened one corner of Reid's mouth.

Joanna hurriedly moved toward him. "It's all right, Paul. I'd like you to meet Reid O'Connor."

"Reid—" she paused for a fraction of a second, annoyed at her own reluctance to make the introduction "—this is Paul LaValliere."

"I am so pleased to meet you at last." Paul offered his hand with his usual courteous Gallic charm. "Thank you for helping Joanna out. It is most generous of you."

After a short pause, Reid shook the proffered hand, an ironic smile curving his lips. "It seems I had no choice."

Paul nodded gravely. "It's a very awkward situation, no?" Then he added with a shrug, "But what's to be done?"

There seemed to be no answer to the question. For a few tense moments, an awkward silence reigned.

Joanna felt disoriented seeing them standing there together: Paul, so polished and well-bred, his dark hair already graying at the temples in a way that made him look even more distinguished; and Reid, tough and down-to-earth, radiating an uncompromising masculinity.

No. No, she couldn't, and wouldn't fall into the trap of comparing them. They were very different men.

Reid finally cleared his throat and shot her a hard look. "I'm sure you're on your way home and I won't keep you very long, but I'd like to have a word with you. It's important."

She took a deep, fortifying breath. Hadn't she been anticipating this moment on pins and needles? They might as well get it over and done.

With a smile, she turned to Paul. "You go ahead. I'll be fine."

He leaned forward to kiss her on the cheek, then drew back and looked down into her face with a small smile. His eyes were filled with love and concern, filled with trust. "I'll see you tomorrow. Be careful driving home."

"I will," she murmured, feeling uncomfortable in front of Reid with Paul's arm still around her.

Then he turned to Reid, who stood with his hands in his pockets watching them impassively, but something in the quirk of his lips told her he'd noticed Paul's proprietary gesture and was amused by it.

"Goodbye, and thanks once again for helping Joanna."

Reid shrugged off the thanks with a small smile.

"I'll see you out." Nervously, she moved toward the door, Paul's arm still around her.

Surely he must feel this disturbing electricity vibrating through her? But if Paul was aware of it he gave no sign. With a peck on the lips, he murmured, "I'll call you tomorrow," then walked out the door.

He was gone. Leaving her alone, in the dark gallery. Alone with Reid.

Suddenly she felt deeply afraid of her own uncontrollable response to him. But there was no escape from that feeling and she knew her only defense was to hide that response as thoroughly as she could.

"I imagine you're angry, but I had no choice. You were avoiding me again."

"I was busy."

Even in the dimly lit space, he could see the cool, wary look in her eyes and felt annoyed.

"Too busy to talk about arranging your mother's release? I called you yesterday, I left five messages. I had to go ahead and make the arrangements without you. Now I just need you to sign these." He pulled the folded papers from his jacket pocket.

Joanna glanced at them, but didn't take them. "What are they?"

"The hospital release forms."

"Aren't you taking too much on yourself?" Her mouth compressed in annoyance.

"No. Your mother called me," he said, and gave her a brief, apologetic smile. "She wants to get out as soon as possible and she asked me to take care of it."

"She asked *you?*" Her voice sharpened. "Why didn't she ask me?"

He could understand her resentment. After all, she'd been carrying this burden on her own until now. On the other hand, she'd also been stalling.

"Maybe because I don't mollycoddle her," he said mildly.

A faint pink flush spread over her cheeks. "I don't either."

He watched as she wrapped her arms across her body in one sharp, jerky movement. It was very obvious that she found it uncomfortable being around him, that she didn't want him here.

The realization hardened his voice. "You do. Stop treating her as if she's going to drop dead any minute."

"What if we take her out of the hospital and something happens? Something we can't cope with?"

"Then we take her back again. Even the doctor agrees she's come as far as she can in the hospital. What are you waiting for? Bring her home."

She turned her head away with a brief, wild laugh. "Home?"

"That's it, isn't it? You'd keep your mother in hospital just to delay this charade that *you're* responsible for." He was beginning to get really impatient with her selfishness.

Her gaze whipped back to him again. "Of course not!"

But a telltale scarlet flush spread over her pale skin, rising up from the scooped neck of the narrow black dress to flood her cheeks.

So the thought of being with him was that abhorrent to her? He couldn't stop the bitterness and anger from showing, and right now he didn't really care what she made of it. "I thought you'd grown up."

Her amber eyes blazed. "Who cares what you think? I don't."

"That's obvious," he muttered, then felt annoyed with himself for letting her goad him. "I didn't come here to argue. Just sign these." He held out the sheaf of forms.

She looked at them for a moment, then took them from his hand with a resentful sniff. She walked over to a small antique writing desk tucked in a corner near the door, and took a pen from the drawer. After giving the forms a cursory glance, she signed each copy. She didn't look at him until she handed back the papers.

He glanced down at her flowing signature and felt a surge of resentment. "One small step for mankind. One giant step for Joanna . . . *Clooney?*" He emphasized the name with a wry, humorless grin and couldn't help adding, "That was an easy mistake to fix."

Her cheeks drained of color and there was a tension around her lips, but she did not respond.

Silence closed around them like a cocoon. In the shadowy interior of the gallery he was achingly aware of her nearness. His head swam with her presence; her subtle perfume wrapped around him and filled his senses as if they were enclosed in a world of their own. It was too private, almost claustrophobic.

"I've had a long day," she said abruptly, her voice husky and a little strained. "I'd really like to go home now."

Beyond that alienating sheen of sophistication lay a hint of vulnerability that he found disturbing. But there was nothing vulnerable about Joanna, he had to remember that. She was just very good at getting her own way.

"One more thing." He deliberately made his voice firm and impersonal. "I went ahead and booked that cottage I mentioned in one of my many messages. We've got it for June and July."

"Unbook it," she said swiftly. "I have no intention of being buried in the middle of nowhere for a couple of months. And as for a nurse, I've been doing interviews all week."

"Have you found anyone yet?"

Her gaze ran over his expressionless face. He just watched her, his hands resting lightly on his narrow hips.

"No." With a slow shake of her head, she turned away. Just looking at him hurt.

"Then come and meet Thelma Crippen—"

"Thelma?" Amusement briefly alleviated her misery. "You want me to entrust my mother to the care of someone named Thelma?"

He frowned, confused. "It's a little old-fashioned, but I don't see what her name has to do with . . ."

"Don't you get it? *Thelma and Louise?*"

A brief grin lit his face. "Oh, yes I see. Well, don't worry about Mrs. Crippen, she's as solid as they come, nothing flighty about her. She won't go driving off any cliffs, or shooting anybody. I faxed you her credentials, they're excellent. I think you'll like her."

"Maybe," she conceded unwillingly. "But this cottage thing is out of the question."

There was no way she could do it. Two months alone with him, playing the part of his loving wife? Her mother would be no protection. No, she couldn't do it.

"Would you rather be at home, trying to explain to everyone you know that you're lying to your mother about your marital status, and could everyone please agree to lie to her too?"

"I get the picture," she said, cutting him off abruptly.

Suddenly it all crowded in on her, the magnitude of this lie she had told, and all of its repercussions. Her shoulders sagged with the enormity of it all. The worst of it was, he was right. The only way to pull off something like this was away from everybody and everything.

"Also the peace and quiet will do her good. Maybe you, too," he added softly.

She quickly glanced over at him, but there was no softness in his face. It was hard and guarded, the creases beside his mouth deeply etched.

"I'm not doing this for me," she said tightly, feeling as if a painful band were constricting her chest. "When are we leaving to go up north?" She felt a little numb.

"How about next Friday at noon?"

"That sounds fine. I'll be ready." She kept her eyes on the gleaming, bare oak floor, unwilling to look at him, afraid he'd see the pain she could not hide.

Suddenly his warm, hard fingers closed around hers. "Joanna."

His voice was deep, husky and gentle, and brought sudden, scalding tears to her eyes. He stepped around in front of her, but she kept her gaze fixed on the pearly-white buttons of his shirt.

With a gentle fingertip he lifted her chin and examined her face. A small frown made a crease between his brows. "Look, all hard feelings aside, are you sure you want to go through with this? It's not too late to tell your mother the truth, you know."

A breathless, poignant yearning filled her for what she'd lost. At this moment he was the old Reid, the man she'd fallen in love with, gentle and kind. How much she had missed his strength, his tenderness. She needed that now, but it wouldn't last.

Grimly, she shook her head. "No! We have to go through with it."

"I don't think you'll be able to do it. I think the strain of the pretense will get to you."

"No more than it'll get to you."

He looked skeptical and shook his head. "She'll see right through you. You haven't been very convincing so far."

"Don't worry about me, I can put on an act just as well as you can."

"This I can hardly wait to see."

He grinned with genuine amusement, and suddenly she just couldn't stand it, couldn't stand the frustration one more second.

"Then what do you think of this performance?" She closed the distance between them and clutched the edges of his leather jacket. Her thumbs smoothed over his chest and she could feel the warmth of his body through the fine oxford-cloth shirt.

He started back in surprise as she leaned up to him and whispered, "Till next Friday, darling."

Something hot and dark flared in his eyes, but she didn't give herself time to analyze it as she reached up and covered his mouth with her own.

For a moment he tensed as her palms skimmed slowly under the edges of the jacket and over the hard contours of his shoulders. But when she slid her tongue along the firm line of his lips, a shudder rippled through him. Taking his bottom lip between her teeth, she sucked it slowly before once again sliding her tongue insistently along his lips until his mouth opened.

Fire singed every nerve, her whole body burned for him. Her senses were flooded with his warmth and the intoxicating smell of his flesh as his tongue languorously entwined with hers. She closed her eyes and gave herself over to bliss, anticipating the euphoria she had always found in his arms, but something was missing. In spite of his surrender, she could sense his restraint.

Then his hands slid up to grasp her arms and he broke the kiss, and held her away from him.

Her eyes snapped open and she stiffened. Had she completely lost her mind? There was no use pretending to herself that she'd kissed him to prove herself capable of the charade. She'd done it to try and alleviate her pent-up desire, and something had gone disastrously wrong. Now she felt even more frustrated, and even worse, mortified. But she didn't have to let him see it.

Abruptly, she pushed away from him. With trembling hands, she smoothed her dress before looking up into his face. "Was that sufficiently wifely?"

Even in the dim light she could see a faint flush staining his cheeks, but otherwise Reid looked calm and composed. "Quite."

"Good. I'll see you next week."

Somehow she managed to turn and walk toward the door, even though her legs were shaking. She held it open for him and waited until he passed through before shutting it and turning the lock. But not once did she look at him. She just couldn't.

Now she was in real trouble.

That illicit, misrepresented demonstration had just burst the floodgates of desire wide open. And Reid had responded, in spite of his restraint. But the thought gave her no sense of triumph. While she fought a gamut of mixed-up emotions, all he had to guard against was, at best, a lukewarm lust.

5

NO SEVEN DAYS of Joanna's life had ever flown by so quickly as the week after Reid came to the gallery. It seemed she'd scarcely blinked before she found herself nearing the end of the long drive into the rugged highlands of eastern Ontario. All too soon she'd have to deal with seeing him again.

Rounding a tight curve in the narrow gravel road that cut through the woods, Joanna suddenly saw the cottage straight ahead of her.

Nestled among dark pines and shaded by a canopy of birches and maples, the rough-hewn timbers of the house were stained a rich chestnut brown that blended into the surrounding forest. In the clearing beside it stood Reid's car.

Her pulse accelerated as she eased into a spot next to the Jag, then switched off the engine.

The sudden silence hit her as she got out of the car and stared at the house, dappled with the long shadows of the summer evening and looking beguilingly peaceful.

Well, here she was. No turning back now. No avoiding the moment she dreaded so much.

Reid had driven up from Toronto earlier in the day, bringing her mother and the nurse, Thelma, in the comfort of the larger car. Pleading a last-minute meeting with the gallery manager, Joanna had been able to put off coming until the late afternoon. Privately, she hadn't even considered going with them.

She'd need her car to go into the city on occasion to check on the gallery. And besides, spending the entire summer here with Reid would be bad enough, but it would be impossible without her own transportation. *Or is that means of escape?* a little voice inside her taunted.

Despite her cowardly desire to delay the inevitable, she hadn't even managed to get lost on the three-hour drive from the city.

Had Reid chosen this area deliberately? She knew he'd grown up somewhere around the nearby town of Bancroft. He had been an only child, and his mother had died when Reid was twelve. He'd been raised by his father, a government geologist, but he too had died before she and Reid ever met.

Apart from those bare facts Reid had always resisted her attempts to get him to talk about his background. He'd always insisted there was nothing to tell. She had suspected there was more to it, but back then it hadn't seemed important. But it was surprising, considering how he'd avoided anything to do with his origins, that he'd choose to come here.

Leaning her hands on the smooth, warm metal of the Porsche's roof for support, she shuddered, and her knees felt a little weak. How on earth was she going to manage being alone with him, sleeping in the same bed with him again, without revealing how she felt?

Don't think about it, just do it. She would take it one day at a time—and pray that the time would pass quickly.

She pushed away from the car and squared her shoulders. After all, hadn't she'd weathered much worse than this?

Leaving her luggage to collect later, she set off along the rough path skirting what was obviously the back of the house. She noticed with pleasure that a wide screened-in porch ran along the length of the building and down one side, perfect for sitting out in the evening. Turning the corner, she caught her breath at the view.

Jack's Lake spread out before her, a small blue gem, sparkling in the late-evening sun. Where the woods had been cleared to build the cottage, outcroppings of pink and gray granite pushed through the thin grassy covering of soil and then became a smooth expanse of rock that sloped gently down into the water. Farther along the shore lay a golden crescent of sandy beach and on either side the trees rustled in the light breeze, each leaf sharp and brilliant in the last slanting beams of the dying day.

Turning down a path that led through the trees to the shoreline, she drank in the beauty, her hand shading her eyes from the blinding ball of fire sinking below the dark pines that crowned towering pink granite cliffs on the opposite shore. There were no other cottages to be seen, not another sign of human habitation.

As she turned to walk back toward the cottage, she realized that her tension had vanished, as if the serene beauty surrounding her had soothed her jangled nerves.

Inhaling deeply of the pine-scented breeze, she could feel herself getting stronger with every step she took. Yes, she could do this. For her mother she could face anything, even Reid.

As she emerged from the shadow of the trees, he was suddenly there in front of her. Walking barefoot, his hands pushed into the pockets of khaki shorts riding low on his narrow hips, and his tanned chest bare, he looked lean and hard and unbearably sexy.

Peace and serenity fled. Tension prickled between her shoulder blades and a surge of desire made her knees weaken.

"You made it all right," he murmured soberly. A small smile curved his lips, but his eyes were guarded.

He stepped closer, put his arms around her and drew her to his bare chest. Her breath caught in her throat. In growing panic, she pushed against him, but his grip tightened.

"Relax," his low, hard voice murmured in her ear. "We have an audience."

She looked past him up toward the cottage. A low-railed cedar deck projected from the front, with an umbrella-shaded picnic table and a cluster of lounge chairs. Behind the deck, the front wall of the cottage itself was almost entirely glass. Two figures were watching them from the picture window. Smiling happily, her mother gave a small wave of welcome—or was it encouragement?

Joanna forced herself to stand, still and submissive, while Reid covered her mouth, his lips warm, hard and

angry against hers. But she couldn't help the involuntary, painfully acute shiver of desire that raced through
her. She managed to stifle the small gasp that rose in her
throat, but couldn't help sagging against him as her eyes
fluttered closed and her lips softened under his.

Then he pushed her away, but kept one hard arm
curved around her shoulders. Her shaking legs seemed
to move of their own volition as they headed toward the
cottage. All she could focus on was fighting back the
molten heat that flooded her body at his touch.

"Come on, come on . . . stop acting like a zombie," he
muttered. "You won't fool anybody like this."

She didn't blame him for being annoyed. After all,
she'd put him in a lousy situation, but he didn't have to
kiss her like *that*. A peck on the cheek would have satisfied their audience just fine.

"If you ever force me to kiss you again, the only thing
that'll feel good to you will be an ice pack. Got it?"

"Ouch!" He winced. "Loud and clear."

Then suddenly he grinned at her, and the wicked,
genuine amusement in his face made him heart-stop-
pingly sexy. "But *force!* Really Joanna, aren't you exag-
gerating a little? Did I force you to lean against me and
close your eyes?"

"I did not!"

"You did." His knowing smile was smug. "Want to
know how I know?"

"Please, do tell." Her sarcasm might be unconvincing, but it was the best she could. She felt cornered.

"You have this little sigh, a movement of your body. You always do it when you close your eyes." A sly smile lurked around his mouth, daring her to deny the truth.

"I'm glad you've arrived. I was beginning to get worried." Her mother's voice came flutingly down from the deck above, the most welcome sound Joanna had ever heard.

She turned abruptly away from the uncomfortably shrewd gleam in Reid's gray eyes. Taking the two steps up onto the deck in a single stride, she went straight into her mother's outstretched arms.

"I'm sorry, I didn't mean to worry you," Joanna murmured and hugged her tightly. Under the smart linen trousers and loose silk shirt, her mother still felt alarmingly thin.

Her mother held her at arm's length and gave her an admonishing look. "What kept you? You said you'd be here by two and it's almost nine. I was ready to call the police, but Reid said he thought he knew what had delayed you, and not to worry."

Joanna glanced back as Reid came up the steps behind her. To her annoyance, he had a knowing smirk on his lips. She flushed uncomfortably. Yes, he knew all right—that she'd been stalling.

"And as you can see, he was right." She turned back to her mother with a reassuring smile. "Here I am, safe and sound." But darting a glance at Reid, she caught the flash of mockery in his eyes.

"Okay, so now everybody's happy. Are you finally ready to go for your walk? Before it gets too dark to see?"

The voice was a dry, prosaic monotone. Joanna turned to see the hired nurse, dressed for duty in a pale green uniform and sturdy walking shoes, stepping through the screen door and out onto the deck.

"You must be Thelma. I'm Joanna. It's nice to meet you."

"Yeah." The nurse's eloquent shrug of resignation implied that she'd lived too long to feel any need for meaningless social chitchat. "Now you're finally here, maybe we can get on with our therapy."

Thelma was a small, wiry woman, with tight salt-and-pepper curls framing her weathered face, and her small black eyes were uncomfortably penetrating. Right now she stood with her arms akimbo, impatience twisting her thin lips.

"I'm sorry, have I been keeping you from your routine?" Joanna flushed, guilty and embarrassed. She couldn't help darting a quick look at Reid and saw his smirk. He'd guessed that the woman already intimidated the hell out of her.

"Naturally she wouldn't go anywhere till *you* arrived," Thelma's flat voice continued.

Joanna could feel her cheeks flaming at the nurse's well-aimed criticism. She should have called to say she'd be late. "I'm sorry..." she stammered out.

"Why don't you and Louise go for your walk now, Thelma?" Reid interpolated smoothly. She shot him a grateful look for coming to her rescue. He was looking at the nurse, but he had a gleam of amusement in his eyes.

He was enjoying himself hugely at her expense. "I'll help my wife get settled in."

My wife. He was really rubbing it in with that cozy, proprietary tone, but she owed him this little revenge. If these subtle taunts were the worst he'd resort to, she would consider herself lucky.

But when his warm hand came to rest possessively on the small of her back, a shudder of tension raced up her spine, even as slow, insidious heat seeped from his fingertips, through her silky rayon dress and into her skin. If it was revenge he was looking for, he was getting it in spades. Thank God he didn't know it. Yet.

"I don't need any help," she protested, a little too sharply. "I can manage."

"Don't be silly, darling. You've had a long drive. I'm sure you must be tired." His warm, rich voice and smile held the lazy contentment of a man who had everything he could desire.

She suppressed a bitter grimace. *Of course he looks pleased with himself. He's got your neck on the chopping block.*

"Joanna, you have a good husband." Her mother smiled adoringly up at Reid, patting his shoulder as she passed by.

He shot her a smug, sidelong glance. Joanna felt a surge of resentment, sharpened by the fact that even when Reid was being insufferable, she found him so damn appealing.

"Yes, he's one of a kind, all right."

Her sarcasm only made him smile. "Come on, sweetheart," he crooned, oozing charm. "I'll show you where we're going to sleep."

His wolfish grin was downright threatening, but somehow it gave her strength and confidence. There was only one way to deal with the situation—fight fire with fire.

Gritting her teeth, she smiled back for her mother's benefit and said lightly, "Thank you, darling."

She watched Thelma help her mother slowly down the wooden steps. Just wait till she got the snake alone. If he was going to play this cat-and-mouse game with her, she was going to make his life hell on earth. Only problem was, she hadn't figured out how to do that. He was so impervious to her.

"Shall we start with the cottage first?" Giving her a bland smile, he held open the screen door, waiting for her to enter.

Alone with Reid once again, she watched with growing trepidation as her mother and Thelma disappeared up the dirt road. Lord knows, she had to be on her guard now. He knew how to read her feelings only too well.

Slowly she walked past him, into the cottage, then stopped with a gasp of surprise. Instantly charmed, she looked around what was obviously the main room, a combination living/dining area and her wariness vanished. "This is wonderful!"

She hadn't come here expecting anything except to feel uncomfortable being isolated with Reid. She'd given no particular thought to the place itself. But this was a de-

lightful surprise. Large windows made up three sides of
the living area, bringing the outside in—a view of green
trees, blue lake and the fiery sunset bathing the room in
an orange glow.

And what a room! A browser's dream.

By the far window stood a big old oak dining table
with four matching chairs. An overstuffed sofa and chair
upholstered in red cut-velvet made a cozy grouping by
the fireplace and a huge antique iron stove occupied the
opposite wall. And no matter where her eye turned, she
found every shelf, every nook and cranny filled with
things.

She wandered slowly around the room in awe, scanning the vintage ads tacked up on the paneled walls. Rock
samples covered the broad mantel of the huge fieldstone
fireplace—sparkling amethyst geodes and ancient fos-
sils. From one rafter hung a collection of hats, among
them a top hat, a bobby's helmet and an ancient bowler.

There were stuffed and mounted fish, horse bridles,
even a pair of dueling pistols. On one wall stood an old
Victorian sideboard, its shelves filled with antique tins
and colorful teapots, old trinkets and souvenirs. Framed
photos were tucked away among all the fascinating junk.

"This place is wonderful! Look at all this stuff!" She
crossed the room to a narrow hall and peeked into the
two small bedrooms, then turned impetuously to Reid,
who was standing very still in the center of the room. "I
love it here." She smiled with delight, forgetting to be
guarded.

It was uncanny, but this place felt so right, as if she could belong. She could be completely happy here, exploring and discovering. And painting! How she had once loved to paint, but she hadn't felt the urge to pick up a brush since her mother's accident.

"You . . . you do?"

He stared at her in disbelief. Had he just heard right? He'd expected her to sneer at this houseful of dusty junk. In fact, he'd counted on it to provide a daily reminder of how incompatible they were. Something, anything to keep his unwanted attraction for her in perspective. But she liked it here!

She certainly didn't belong here, no matter what she said. Framed against the weathered boards, she looked cool and crisp and citified in her slim-fitting white dress, exuding the sexiness that was part of her without even trying. Whether he liked it or not, he still desired her. And now he knew that he still turned her on, whether *she* liked it or not.

He found himself gruffly apologizing. "I'm sorry it's so rustic and inconvenient. You don't have to be polite. If you'd rather, there's a cottage resort not far away. It's got every modern amenity. . . ."

"No, no," she insisted. "This is so beautiful, tucked away from the world, like a piece of heaven." Her face and voice were filled with genuine affection. "How did you ever find it?" Her almond-shaped eyes were dark and mysterious, watching him, making his skin prickle.

"I know the guy who owns it," he said, his defenses badly shaken.

"Is he the one who collected all these interesting things?" She picked up a tin tea caddy from among the motley collection on the old sideboard. That was one of the few pieces of furniture his dad had inherited from his grandmother.

"No, his father did."

"Did you know him too?"

"His name was Jack," he said slowly. "This lake was named after him."

"He must have been a very interesting person. I wish I could have met him."

His mouth curved in a small, humorless smile. "I don't think you would have found him very interesting. He was just a dreamer, a rambler. A country bumpkin by your standards."

"What makes you think I wouldn't have found him interesting?"

"He wasn't sophisticated."

She shook her head impatiently. "As if I'd care about that."

Of course she'd have cared. And what about her father? For the life of him he couldn't picture their fathers meeting. Jonathan Clooney in his silk cravats and Savile Row suits, and his dad, in his scruffy jeans and worn work boots. Halton wouldn't even have let him through the front door.

Jonathan would have had even more reason to think his daughter was throwing herself away. Reid O'Connor wasn't good enough for the daughter of Jonathan Clooney, the product of four generations of inherited wealth.

She could look much higher for a husband than a working guy who'd hauled himself up by his bootstraps to be the owner of a struggling contracting firm.

His rival for Joanna's loyalty had been her father, a loyalty Jonathan demanded in the name of love and affection. And Daddy had won.

He'd tried so hard to see her, to talk to her, after she left him. But she'd shut herself up in that damn fortress and refused to even hear him out. In true Clooney fashion, she cold-bloodedly eliminated the problem from her life.

When her father had come, on her behalf, and asked him to release Joanna from what he fastidiously called her "youthful folly," that was when he'd finally realized it was over. She couldn't even be bothered to come herself.

Since she clearly didn't love him, there was no point in staying married. He'd accepted Jonathan's offer to have the family lawyer handle everything if he'd agree to initiate the divorce. So he'd signed the papers and within weeks he was a free man. Free, and smarter.

He clenched his jaw tight. He'd never let himself be jerked around by her again. Then why was he so edgy? He forced the muscles in his face to relax.

He'd thought that he'd be able to do this, even thought of it as a way to prove to Joanna that he was man enough to let bygones be bygones, and do the right thing by Louise. If only he'd realized how hard that would be. Still, chances were that once he got tonight over with, it would be easier.

All day he'd been on edge about sharing that cabin with her. But he had to stay calm and cool. He couldn't afford to expose his wayward libido, but some responses were hard to hide, and it was a very small cabin.

He gritted his teeth and deliberately pushed away the images that thought provoked. What was he worried about? He wasn't an animal. He could control himself. And he wouldn't let her make a fool of him again.

He turned away and headed briskly for the door. "Come on, I'll show you around the rest of the place."

His sudden abruptness left her confused. What had she done? She wished she could read him as easily as he could read her.

She followed him out the door and down the steps, trotting to keep up with his long stride. A glance at his face showed once again a clenched look, and that small, telltale pulse beating at the corner of his mouth. Under her breath, she heaved a sigh of despair.

For a while there she'd thought they were starting to get along. They were talking to each other, and she'd felt at ease with him for the first time. But now all that tension and restraint were back. Still, perhaps it was better this way, safer.

Reid led her down through the trees along a narrow, hilly path that skirted the lake, until they came to a small log hut, nestled in a dip of the rocks and out of sight of the cottage.

He threw open the door and muttered gruffly, "The flue's broken on the stove, so unfortunately you'll have to wait until I get it fixed before you can use the sauna."

Joanna peered into the cedar-paneled, windowless room with its broad-slatted bench and small iron stove. The water lapped only a foot or two away from the door, and it was tempting to imagine plunging into the cold water, all hot and tingling from a sauna with Reid. Tempting, but not smart.

"That's all right," she said quickly. "I'm not much of a sauna person."

He shrugged as if he didn't much care, and strode off across the rocks to the little beach. Joanna hurried after him along the shore to a square redwood structure sitting right on the water, with a wooden dock extending fifteen feet out into the lake.

He opened the windowed door to show her the interior of the boathouse. "There's a couple of canoes here and anything else you might need."

She stepped inside, and found the air hot and still and faintly musty. Near the door an L-shaped workbench stretched along two of the walls, with tools neatly hung above it. A battered old red canoe lay upside down on the farther side, beside a newer, cedar-strip craft. Life jackets were piled in one corner and paddles mounted on wall brackets above.

At the far end of the workbench, she noticed an ancient record player and went over to have a closer look at the stack of 78s lying beside it. She smiled with pleasure to find a treasure trove of forties and fifties classics—Frank Sinatra, Patsy Cline, Sam Cooke, The Platters.

Reid had remained just outside the door. "I'll go get your bags and show you where we're going to sleep."

Perplexed, she turned to look after him as he went stiffly away. Why on earth was he suddenly so angry and resentful? She'd told him how much she liked this place.

With a sigh, she replaced the pile of disks and walked out of the boathouse to the edge of the dock. She sank down on the sun-warmed boards, leaned her chin on her knees and wrapped her arms tightly around herself. Listening to the soft rippling noises around her, she watched the stars come out one by one, tiny sparkles in the darkening sky.

All around her, the still water shimmered like glass, a pale fuchsia mirror in the fading light. In spite of the beauty of the evening a sense of doom filled her. Why was she so worried? Everything was going to work out fine. Reid might be angry with her, but he cared about her mother. He was a decent man. He had integrity. But it wasn't Reid she was worried about, it was herself.

A slender crescent moon was rising in the east and all that remained of the setting sun was a fiery sliver of crimson on the western horizon. The bloodred light bathed the trees on the farther shore, making the scene look like a Maxfield Parrish painting.

Suddenly the colors fragmented before her eyes, and hot tears flowed slowly down her cheeks. Impatiently, she wiped them away with the back of her hand. *Damn Maxfield Parrish!* He always made her cry.

At the sound of footfalls on the rocks, she quickly brushed at her wet face. The last thing she needed was for him to see her tears.

"Come on, I'll show you where we're going to sleep."

She turned and looked up to see him standing on the rocky ground above the boathouse, holding her bags in his hands. Without waiting for a reply, he turned and walked away. With that feeling of doom weighing on her even more heavily, she followed.

Almost hidden by the trees, a small white cabin lay up ahead, about a hundred feet from the main cottage.

Reid was already there, waiting for her to catch up. With his hands full of her cases, he shouldered open the door. "It isn't much, but it's home."

Joanna stopped on the threshold, a wave of cold dread creeping up her spine as she scanned the tiny room. It was barely large enough to accommodate two dressers, a small pine wardrobe and the bed—the piece of furniture that seemed to dominate the small space.

She looked down at the futon on a low wooden frame. With plump pillows and crisp lace-edged sheets, topped by a downy-soft white duvet, it looked inviting, brand-new and completely out of place. A bed that looked as if it were made for much more than just sleeping in.

Had he done this just for her? The thought warmed her, but at the same time a sudden erotic image filled her head, of sinking down into that softness with Reid's naked body wrapped around her.

Swallowing hard, she felt heat flooding through her, tightening her nipples against the soft fabric of her dress and pooling between her thighs to throb unbearably. All at once she could hardly breathe.

"It's very nice." Her husky voice cracked. She hurriedly cleared her throat and took a deep shuddery breath. "As a matter of fact, this whole place is very nice. Thank you for all the obvious trouble you've taken to make it comfortable."

"I'm glad you approve." Reid's face was very serious, the lines beside his mouth deeply etched.

She hardly knew what she said. "I think it'll be great for Mom."

"And you? Will this be good for you too?"

That was the second time he'd asked her something like that, but she'd be a fool to think it meant he cared.

"I'm not the one who needs it." She picked up her largest case and tossed it onto the bed. She desperately needed something to do, something to distract her from his probing gaze, from the unwanted sensations tormenting her.

"Are you sure about that?"

"Of course I'm sure! What do you mean?" She unzipped the case with shaky fingers and flipped it open.

Why wouldn't he get out of here? His presence in the small cabin was too overpowering. Standing barely a foot away, he was watching her with that steady, all-seeing gaze that burned right into her.

"I mean that you're tense and edgy and you look tired."

"And you think I'll be able to relax here?" She couldn't keep the sarcasm, or the edge of hysteria from her voice as she turned to face him.

For a long moment he just looked at her, a hard, dispassionate expression darkening his eyes. When he spoke, his tone was matter-of-fact. "You still want me."

The bald statement made her gasp. But when she opened her mouth to deny it, no words came out. Her cheeks burned and she could only stare at him, at the scorn in his eyes.

"Don't worry, you don't have to qualify that. I got your message loud and clear. I'm still the uncouth guy from the wrong side of the tracks." There was nothing pleasant in his cold smile. "But that's what turns you on, isn't it, Joanna?"

Every inch of her was trembling, trembling with helpless need, with the pain of his rejection. Somehow she found her voice. Somehow she made it hard and cold. "If you think I'm going to share this cabin with you, you can think again."

"I *know* you're going to share this cabin with me." Reid sounded just as hard, and utterly remorseless. "You started this stupid charade, now you're going to go through with it." He stepped closer, his eyes blazing with intensity. "Did you really think it would be that easy?"

"No, I didn't think it would be easy," she said quietly, calmly, but anger rose inside her to simmer just below the surface. "Have you finished rubbing my nose in it?"

The fire slowly died in his eyes, leaving bored resignation behind. That look she dreaded above all.

"You can stop worrying. We won't be sharing a bed. I have my standards . . . and a sleeping bag." He pointed to the navy blue roll in the corner. "However, you are going to have to put up with me being in the same room."

He stepped over and opened the door. "You've made your bed, now you'll have to lie in it."

"At least I don't have to lie in it with you," she threw back sharply.

"What are you trying to do, cheer me up?" Suddenly a grin lit his face that thoroughly disarmed her.

Where had all that anger gone? Anxiously, she searched the carefree, almost boyish expression. Then she saw it. Deep in his eyes lay something grim and implacable. No, the anger wasn't gone, just buried. For now.

He went out, closing the door quietly behind him.

Her shoulders slumped and her head felt as heavy as if it were filled with lead. The situation was hopeless. Like it or not, Reid was right. She'd been caught in a trap of her own making, now she had to find the courage to deal with it.

6

THE SCREEN DOOR squeaked as Joanna opened it and paused on the threshold of the cottage. Her gaze went straight to Reid, sitting on the sofa. He was looking at her with the shuttered expression that made her self-conscious and uncomfortable.

"Hi honey, are you all unpacked?" Her mother's voice called out from across the room where she and Thelma were seated at the dining table playing cards.

She gave her mother a strained smile. "All done."

She scrupulously avoided looking at Reid, as she crossed the room to stand by the old round table. Yet she was aware when he shifted restlessly against the old sofa cushions, and tried to quell the unwelcome tremor of desire that made her skin prickle.

"What do you think about your sleeping cabin?" Her mother smiled up at her, unconscious of the tension that filled the air between Joanna and Reid. "Isn't that the cutest little thing you ever did see?"

"It certainly is little." She tried to give a teasing laugh, but her voice came out too husky and strained.

Shifting her gaze, she noticed Thelma watching her. There was something disturbingly astute about those small black eyes. Joanna wondered nervously how much they saw and what Thelma would say to Louise.

"Don't think of it as small—it's cozy." Her mother peered over at Reid with a knowing gleam in her eyes. "That's what you two kids need, I suspect, the time and place to cozy up to each other."

That was the last thing she wanted. The muscles in her stomach tightened into a hard, painful knot. It wasn't surprising that her mother suspected all was not well in their "marriage." She couldn't have done a worse job of acting naturally if she'd tried.

"Go on, Joanna." With a roguish twinkle in her eyes, Louise gave an encouraging nod in Reid's direction. "Go cuddle up to your husband. He's sitting there all alone and looking a little left out."

No! She was determined to put up a better front than she had so far, but she couldn't face putting on that kind of performance right now. Not so soon.

Suddenly Reid surged to his feet. "I have a better idea." Crossing the room toward the door, he said over his shoulder, "Let's go out to dinner. You haven't eaten yet, have you, hon?"

Was that as in *Attila*? Watching him take his jacket from the hook, she said dubiously, "Out? Where?"

He shrugged into the cream-colored windbreaker. "We're not that far from Bancroft. We can be there in fifteen minutes. I'll show you around town."

"What a lovely idea." Her mother sounded delighted. "Give you two kids a chance to be alone."

"You make it sound too exciting for words," Joanna said with a wry grimace.

Reid stepped into the light, and the annoyance on his face made her regret the crack. He'd made the suggestion to get them out of an awkward situation, not because he wanted to go out with her.

OVERHEAD THE SKY glowed a deep translucent blue, but it was getting dark under the trees as they drove away from the cottage, down the narrow, bumpy road through the woods.

In the dim interior, she turned her head and surreptitiously studied Reid's profile as he concentrated on negotiating the twisting track.

"Thanks for rescuing us. I'm afraid I was a little ungracious back there."

"Don't thank me. I wasn't up to putting on the husband-and-wife act for your mother."

She took a deep breath and decided to go out on a limb. "I think we should look at this evening as an opportunity to put things on a more comfortable footing between us." And perhaps make the coming night easier to cope with.

He shot her a skeptical look, but made no comment. She quickly turned her head to stare out through the windshield at the rocks and brush picked out of the faint evening mist by the headlights' glare.

Reid slowed the car as they reached the junction, and turned right onto the tarmac road that presumably led toward town.

His pointed silence made her rush into speech again. "Despite everything that's happened and how we feel about each other, I very much want to put the past behind us and start fresh. Surely by now whatever animosity we felt can be dispensed with. We can start getting to know each other as—" she hesitated over the word, but plunged ahead "—as *friends?*"

His impatient expulsion of breath spoke volumes.

She went on hurriedly, "All right, maybe friends is the wrong word. How about allies? After all, whether we like it or not, we're in this together. It's equally difficult for both of us, but it would be so much easier if we could just try to put our grievances aside and get along."

"I suppose you have a point. After all, it might help to be united against your mother's attempts to cozy us up together."

So they had a truce. But could she be friends with Reid? He already knew that she wanted him, but he didn't have to know how hard it was for her to fight the desire.

Before she could think about it, she stuck out her hand toward him. "Let's shake on it then."

He glanced down at her hand, up to her eyes, then back to the road ahead. His mouth curved in ironic amusement, but at the same time he reached out and took her hand in a brief, hard grip.

A sharp electric sensation tingled in her arm long after he'd let go. Why him? What was it about Reid that drew her to him inexorably, in spite of his indifference, in spite of everything?

She lowered the window and took a deep breath of the cool evening air. She felt drugged by the close proximity of Reid. The breeze blowing on her face helped to clear her head and steady her.

They passed a gas station and a lone farm and at last the sign reading Welcome to Bancroft became visible up ahead.

Reid slowed to a crawl as the road began to slope downward. The town lay nestled in a bowl of rugged hills, their peaks catching the last wash of pale light.

"There's the old railway station. It's now the Mineral Museum." He waved off to the left and she leaned forward to get a better look as they drifted past a long, one-story white building with a steeply sloped roof. "That's Bancroft's big claim to fame—being the mineral capital of Canada," he said offhandedly.

This was where Reid had grown up. It was part of who he was. Not for the first time she realized how little she knew about the man she'd married. But here was an opportunity to learn more.

She leaned forward eagerly, pointing to a log house a little farther down the hill. "And what's that over there?"

"The historical museum. They think the smaller part of the building could go back to the eighteen-fifties."

"Was your family here for a long time?"

"No," he said lightly, "just a good time. Great-grampa O'Connor was the most successful bootlegger in town."

"Yeah, right. And I was born yesterday."

At the bottom of the hill the road crossed a bridge. Railings obscured the view and she couldn't get a good look in the dusk. "Did you swim in that river when you were a boy?"

"Nope."

She looked over at him leaning back in his seat, one arm out the window, one hand on the steering wheel, totally unruffled. Obviously she didn't have the same stimulating effect on him as he had on her.

Reaching a T-junction, they turned left onto what appeared to be the main street of the small town. "Most of the village is back that way," he said lazily, jerking a thumb over his shoulder. "But everything's closed now except for a few convenience stores. And the bars, of course."

"Do you ever go into any of those bars?"

"Sometimes."

She smothered a sigh. Okay, she didn't need to be hit over the head. He'd play tour guide, but his life wasn't on the itinerary. There'd be no tripping down memory lane. But she'd get him to make conversation if it killed her.

"I was thinking," she began, a little awkwardly, "Maybe after dinner we could stop in at one of those bars. Have a drink or something. Hang out together. It might make this whole ordeal a little easier for both of us."

He glanced over at her, clearly unimpressed.

She reined in her annoyance and made another determined stab at promoting this shaky truce. "Perhaps we could have a beer and a game of pool."

A yelp of laughter burst out of him. "Pool! What do you know about pool?"

"I've played pool!" Indignant, she sat up a little straighter. "We have a table at home, don't you remember?"

"Correction, you've played billiards. Apart from the fact that they're different games, they attract different kinds of people. And your sort are definitely not pool."

She gasped. "You're a snob!"

"*I'm* a snob?" He let out another burst of laughter.

She stared back at him, unamused. He was only doing this to goad her.

"Come on, Joanna, can't you see the irony?" Amusement crinkled the corners of his gray eyes as he glanced at her.

"No, I can't. I'm doing everything I can to put things on a friendlier footing and you're not helping one bit. Now what's wrong with just having a drink together?"

"Nothing," he said more soberly. "But not in one of those bars." He pulled up at a red light.

"Why not?"

For a long moment he just looked at her, frowning, between his brows, his gaze running up over her legs, over the length of her body. When he reached her face, the frown turned to that lazy mockery that was so much a part of him these days. "Because you wouldn't fit in."

"What do you mean?"

"You're a little overdressed."

She looked down at herself. "In this? It's just a simple white dress, for heaven's sakes."

"Yeah, a simple white dress that cost five hundred bucks. But it's more than the dress. It's that silver spoon look you've got."

"What do you mean?"

"The perfect skin, the manicured nails. Everything about you reeks of privilege. It can make other people feel resentful."

She felt a little stab of hurt. "And you just made *me* feel superficial, as if there's nothing more to me than my appearance. Have you always thought so little of me?"

"Don't be so touchy," he said impatiently. "These bars are rough places, Joanna. You'd get hit on from the moment you stepped in the door. And I'm not interested in being beaten to a pulp trying to protect you. We'll just have to do all that bonding stuff in the restaurant."

The light changed to green and he pulled away. They drove in silence for a few minutes until, up ahead, she saw a building set back off the highway. Above the rustic, maple-stained board-and-batten exterior, a green neon dragon glowed incongruously and red letters spelled out Wong's Chinese Restaurant.

Soon Reid was pulling into the only remaining empty space in the graveled parking lot.

"Well, this is obviously quite a popular spot to eat."

Reid gave a dry chuckle. "You could say that. But so is every other restaurant in town on a Friday night."

They crossed the parking lot and he held open the door of the restaurant. As she walked past him, across the threshold, he was so close that his warmth sent a small shiver of desire snaking through her. Ruthlessly, she shoved the unwanted feeling away. She had hoped that getting out of the confined space of the car would make his nearness easier to bear. So far it wasn't working.

Inside, the restaurant glowed with light and echoed with the chatter of people. The large, pleasant room had banquettes around the walls, circular tables in the middle and was filled with the appetizing aroma of good food.

As Joanna stepped into the room, the clatter of cutlery and the babble of voices suddenly stilled. Everyone seemed to turn as one and stare at her.

She stopped dead in the doorway, feeling intensely self-conscious. "I see what you mean," she whispered. "But isn't this a bit ridiculous? It's not as if I've sprouted another head."

When Reid said nothing, she turned to find him looking down at her with an apologetic smile. "They're probably staring at you because you're with me. I never used to come here with female company."

"Not even your fiancée?"

His smile faded and his face tightened a little in annoyance. "No maître d' here, Joanna. You seat yourself." And taking her by the elbow, Reid steered her toward an empty booth at the far end of the room.

"Hi ya, Reid." A man with a ruddy, weather-beaten face nodded to him from one of the tables as they passed by.

"Hey, Sam," he acknowledged casually.

"Who's the lovely lady?" Sam called after him.

Reid turned around, bringing her with him. "This is my wife, Joanna. Joanna, this is Sam Dickson."

Sam looked her over thoroughly, as if deciding whether she measured up. Joanna found herself holding her breath for his judgment. What did it matter? She wasn't even married to Reid anymore! Then he smiled broadly and she felt absurdly pleased that she'd passed muster.

"Well, congratulations," his voice boomed out loudly enough for the whole restaurant to hear. "About time this troublemaker got himself hitched. Do you hear that, everybody?" He raised his voice even louder. "Reid O'Connor went and got himself married!"

Everyone started to applaud and before she knew it they were surrounded by people shaking Reid's hand, kissing her on the cheek and offering their congratulations.

Acutely embarrassed, she submitted to the hearty well-wishers, until at last Reid managed to extricate them politely from the knot of people.

With his hand still curled around her elbow, he steered her toward a booth at the back.

"What did you do that for? Tell him I was your wife?" she whispered, aware that everyone was still watching them.

"I thought it was best to stick to one story," he murmured.

They reached the empty booth and she slid in, sinking comfortably into the red vinyl upholstery. Reid took his seat across from her and handed her one of the menus tucked behind the condiment caddy.

A low, bamboo-shaded lamp shed a pool of muted light on the Chinese-red surface of the Formica tabletop. To her profound relief, the rest of the clientele was losing interest in them and going back to their meals.

A plump blond waitress appeared just as Joanna realized how hungry she was. Not to be left out, she added her profuse congratulations before eventually taking their order.

When she finally departed, Joanna turned to find Reid staring at her. For once there was no hostility or even reserve in his eyes, just curiosity. Under his gaze she could feel slow heat rising inside her, and although it made her feel a little self-conscious, it wasn't an unpleasant feeling in the least.

Needing to break the suddenly loaded silence, she cleared her throat. "What did that man mean when he called you a troublemaker? Were you a bad kid?"

For a moment, she wondered if he was going to avoid her questions again. Then he grinned and shook his head. "Not bad. A little wild maybe. I'm sure you've noticed, there's not much to do in this town. All I wanted to do was get out."

"And you did." Miracle of miracles, he was actually talking to her.

"Yep. As soon as I was finished school."

"And now you're back."

The corner of his mouth quirked in a wry smile. "Which just goes to prove there's no escaping your roots."

"Or your destiny?"

"If you believe in that sort of thing." He shrugged. "Do you?"

She met his eyes directly. "I suppose I must believe. I wouldn't have chosen for my mother to go into a coma and my father to have died." *And the last thing I wanted was for my marriage to end.*

The night she left Reid, she hadn't meant it to be forever. One rash action, meant to shake him up, had gone horribly awry. Before she knew it, she was divorced.

"I'm sorry we never had a chance to talk at the funeral, but you left before I had the opportunity," she said. "I wanted to tell you how much I appreciated your coming, how much it meant to me. I know you and Dad didn't always see eye-to-eye."

"Joanna, I was very sorry to hear about your dad. I knew how devastated you had to be."

She looked up to see genuine sympathy in his eyes. She dropped her gaze to the table again, afraid that sympathy would be her undoing. It was all she could do to nod as she felt a huge lump form in her throat.

"I thought you were surprised to see me," he continued.

"No, I knew you'd come, no matter what had happened between us."

"You did?"

"For all your faults, you're not petty."

"Sure about that? How do you know there isn't a snake in your bed?"

He grinned and she couldn't help smiling back. "I don't. But despite the way you feel about me, and the fact that you don't need our old problems coming back to haunt you, here you are, still doing the decent thing. And I want to thank you."

He shrugged, obviously uncomfortable. "I'd do anything for Louise."

Yes, her mother again. She felt unreasonably let down. But he hadn't come to the funeral for her mother's sake, she reminded herself. "You've proved that, at the cost of a lot of upheaval in your life. This must be very hard on your fiancée."

Something in his eyes switched off. His jaw tightened and now he looked formidably unapproachable. "If you don't mind, I'd rather not bring her into this."

She'd overstepped the bounds of their truce and the intimacy was shattered. It was obvious that he wanted to protect his fiancée from a distasteful situation, protect her by ensuring her privacy. Who was this woman who had the love and loyalty that had once been hers?

Suddenly she became aware of a tinkling of cutlery on glassware that rapidly became a piercing chorus from all corners of the restaurant.

Joanna looked around in confusion to see everyone smiling at them once again. "What are they doing now?"

Reid looked pained. "Think about it. Married. Wedding reception . . ."

Understanding dawned, and she let out a groan. "Oh, no. Not that!"

Now she saw the expectancy in the smiles, and noticed that even the cook had come to the kitchen doorway, and stood there with his massive arms crossed, grinning like a big fool.

Reid said quietly, "You know, they won't give up until we do our duty as bride and groom."

"Then we might as well get it over and done with." Feeling completely trapped, she gave him a tight smile.

He stood, leaned forward over the table and gently lifted her chin. Joanna closed her eyes; she mustn't look at him. Somehow she had to turn off her mind, and even more importantly, turn off her body.

Then his warm, firm lips touched hers, and she had to fight the wave of helpless, eager response sweeping through her. To her shock, his mouth opened on hers and his tongue slowly swept her lips until she parted them for him.

For one mad moment she forgot that they were the focus of this room full of people. The whole world became reduced to the feeling of his tongue and its slow, thorough and devastating exploration of her mouth.

Fortunately, Reid had no problem keeping focused. After a suitable length of time he released her chin and sat back down to wild applause.

"I'm sorry about that kiss. But if we hadn't put on a good show, they'd just keep bugging us."

"That's all right." She was trembling, but somehow, she managed to keep her voice steady. "I imagine it's one of the drawbacks of small-town living. Probably the closest thing they have to dinner theater."

Her face burned with mortification at her inability to control her reaction to his kiss, but when she finally had the courage to look at him she was surprised to see that he too bore a faint flush on his cheekbones. Embarrassment, that was all. She knew better than to think he was affected by *her*. That kiss may have looked hot, but only she knew how passionless it had been—for Reid.

To her intense relief, the waitress arrived with their dinner less than a minute later. As she picked at her Szechwan chicken, they reverted to small talk and Reid remained pleasant, but slightly distant. Yet for the rest of the meal, she couldn't erase the feeling of his lips on hers.

What more did she want from him? He'd promised to make an effort to be civil, and he was keeping his promise.

ONLY THE SOFT chirping of crickets broke the dense silence as they walked to the sleeping cabin. It was only eleven-thirty, but her mother and Thelma had already gone to bed and the cottage lay in darkness behind them.

The weak moonlight didn't penetrate the forest canopy and it was inky black. Reid lit her way with a small flashlight he'd taken from his pocket. Joanna's sandals sank into the soft, slippery mat of evergreen needles and she stumbled more than once on the unfamiliar path. Each time Reid would reach out to steady her with a warm, hard grip on her upper arm. His touch sparked a need for him so strong she could hardly take the next step. She bit down on her lip to overcome that feeling. Considering where they were headed, she couldn't afford to feel that way.

When they reached the darkened cabin, she opened the door and searched for the light switch with cold, nervous fingers.

"Allow me." Reid's deep murmur close behind her sent a shiver racing painfully over the surface of her skin.

He brushed past, she heard a click and saw a small tongue of flame. She watched in dismay as he lit the candles on the wall sconce above the dresser and a warm, mellow glow filled the room. She hadn't even noticed there was no electricity in here. Everything seemed to be conspiring against her, making it impossible to fight her dangerous need.

He replaced the lighter on the dresser, then turned and gave her a sardonic look.

Caught off guard, she was afraid that everything she was feeling must be showing on her face. She only wished the same were true for him. What did he *really* feel about all this?

"I'll be back in a few minutes." Nothing in his voice gave her any indication, either. He went back outside, closing the door quietly behind him.

She sank weakly down onto the futon, undressed mechanically and slipped on her nightshirt. She got into bed, her heart beating a mile a minute and her ears straining to catch the sounds of him out there in the darkness. Where was he? What was he thinking at this moment?

Nothing disturbed the deep silence of the northern night. The breeze had died, leaving no breath of air to rustle the leaves in the trees or stir the water. Just beyond the uncurtained window the lake lay limpid and still, reflecting back the crescent moon hanging dead center in the sky above.

Then she heard the soft crunch of footsteps. Her breath caught in her throat and her heart began to race. She heard the rattle of the doorknob, then the door swinging open with a light creak. He came in, bringing the pine-laden scent of night air and something else, something earthy and dangerous. Something she wanted at this moment more than life itself. Something she couldn't have.

And yet she couldn't resist turning to torment herself with the sight of him. She had to say something to defuse the tension. "Thanks for giving me some privacy."

He gave her a brief, sober look, then turned to place the contents of his pockets on the dresser.

"I didn't do it for you. I did it for me." Although his voice was soft and even, she could sense his restrained tension.

"Well, whatever your reasons, thank you anyway."

He grunted and began undoing his shirt buttons, baring his chest.

No, she couldn't take any more. Rolling over on her side, she turned away from the tormenting sight of him to stare blindly at the wall.

She chewed on her nail, listening to the rasp of his jeans zipper being opened, then the whisper of denim sliding over flesh. She heard the jeans land in the corner with a light thud.

"I've been thinking," she said desperately, to distract herself. "Things could be worse." She chewed harder on her nail, willing herself not to imagine how he looked right now. "If our bedroom was in the cottage . . . Those walls are paper thin . . ."

"And you think that would be worse?"

She made the mistake of turning to look at him. Her heart skipped a beat as her gaze ran over his tall, lean body. Wearing only white briefs that molded his firm buttocks, Reid was reaching to snuff out the candles.

She managed to falter, "Look on the bright side. . . ."

He doused the flames, and the room was dark except for a faint glimmer of moonlight coming through the window. "I'm not sure there is a bright side. I'm not sure we can be friends. I'm not sure we haven't got ourselves in a huge mess." His tired voice clutched at her conscience.

"You mean, *I've* gotten us into a huge mess. Why don't you just say it?" She felt utterly miserable.

"Just go to sleep, Joanna." Reid sounded resigned.

Now that her eyes had adjusted in the weak moonlight, she could see him quite clearly, lying on his sleeping bag not a foot away, between her and the window. The chiseled contours of his face, the rise and fall of his bare chest, the gleam of his white underwear and the silhouette of his muscular thigh against the faint light.

If she reached out, she could touch him. In her sleep she could fling out an arm, a leg, make contact. So close, and yet how far apart they were. She wished she could turn back the hands of time.

Suddenly a tear welled up and trickled down her cheek. She barely managed to bite back a shuddering sob. This was all she needed to make a complete fool of herself. Didn't he think little enough of her already?

But in spite of that, more silent, burning tears came coursing down her cheeks. She'd never felt so alone, so unloved, so uncared for.

And then she felt Reid's hand clasping hers in a warm, comforting grip, and heard the heartbreaking reassurance of his gruff, reluctant voice through the darkness. "Go to sleep, Joanna."

7

JOANNA WOKE to an empty room.

It was eight o'clock, much earlier than she usually got up on a Saturday morning. A brilliant sun was sparkling off the waters of the lake, and the sky above was a glorious shade of blue. A picture-postcard day like this couldn't help but fill her with a certain amount of optimism.

She had gotten through the first night with Reid, and even though it had clearly been just as difficult for him, they had managed. And today she planned to keep out of his way by devoting herself to her mother and giving Thelma the day off. Her confidence went up a notch. Maybe they could get through this thing after all.

She dressed quickly in a pair of denim cutoffs and a white T-shirt, then looked at herself in the mirror and pulled a wry face. Hopefully this outfit would make her look like one of the natives.

She stepped out of the cabin onto rocks still wet with dew. A thin drift of mist hung above the still water of the lake, and the air smelled wonderfully fresh and cool. She made her way carefully over the damp rock to the cottage. The aroma of freshly brewed coffee and baking greeted her as she opened the door and stepped inside.

"Good morning darling, did you sleep well?" Her mother's cheerful smile and the spring in her step made her look almost like her old self as she emerged from the kitchen with a basket of muffins in her hand.

"Very well." Joanna smiled back, marveling that, after only one day here, her mother already seemed more robust. It reaffirmed her feeling of optimism. "And you?"

"Like a top," her mother said perkily, and planted a kiss on Joanna's cheek on her way to the round dining table, where four places had already been laid on the snowy cloth.

Just at that moment, Reid emerged from the hallway which led to the small bathroom. His hair was damp from the shower, and he wore khaki shorts and a loose cotton shirt that clung to his broad shoulders. When his eyes met hers, bright and piercing, they revealed nothing.

She felt a stab of disappointment to find him just as guarded. After his gruff words of sympathy last night, she'd expected him to act more like . . . what? A friend? How foolish of her.

"What are you all waiting for, a formal invitation? Sit down and start eating before the food gets cold."

She was never so glad to hear Thelma's strident voice, as the nurse marched out of the kitchen with a pot of coffee.

Joanna quickly turned away from Reid and moved toward the table, afraid her disappointment would show on her face. But he came up behind her and held out her chair. She looked over her shoulder at him in surprise, and though he held her gaze steadily, his glittering, intense look was still quite impassive. He held out a chair for her mother and Thelma in turn, but she noticed that he smiled in his lazy way at both of them. That abandoned feeling came back to haunt her.

Reid took the seat across from her and looked straight into her eyes. For a moment a look of exasperation crossed his face, then his expression became resigned. He pushed the basket of muffins towards her. "Eat some breakfast."

Absurdly, she felt her spirits rise again. It would be all right. He hadn't forgotten their truce. She tucked into her food as if she hadn't eaten in a month.

After breakfast her mother disappeared into the kitchen and returned carrying a wicker basket. "It's beautiful out there today. Just perfect for a picnic, don't you think?"

Joanna took a sip of her coffee and watched her mother park the basket on the chair next to her. "Are you sure you're up to it, Mom?"

Although clearly feeling stronger this morning, she still had that fragile look. The lines of strain were still evident around her mouth, and her hand trembled slightly as she put down the basket.

"I'm not going. You and Reid are."

Joanna choked on her mouthful of coffee. "What!"

"It's clear to me that the two of you haven't had much time together just having fun."

Joanna darted a glance at Reid, but he looked completely unperturbed as he helped Thelma clear the table.

"But we're up here to be with *you!*" So much for her plan to spend the day avoiding Reid. In spite of their truce, a prolonged period in his company could be very dangerous.

Her mother gave a dismissive little shake of her head. "Don't be ridiculous, Joanna. Go spend the day with your husband."

There was no point in arguing. She knew that from long experience. Once her meddlesome parent set her mind on something, it was impossible to deflect her. "If you're sure you won't mind."

"Of course not, and I won't be lonely, either." She neatly forestalled Joanna's other objection. "I have Thelma."

"And I know the perfect spot," Reid added amiably, clinching the plans.

Joanna looked over at him with an apology in her eyes, but he avoided her gaze as he swiped crumbs off the table.

"I'll get my things," she murmured as she turned away.

"I'll meet you at the car," he said behind her. If he felt any kind of resentment, she couldn't hear it.

"And I don't want to see your faces till sundown!"

Joanna could hear the glee in her mother's voice. Obviously she was happy that her machinations were running so smoothly.

After throwing a few necessities into a bag, Joanna went out to join Reid. He had the Jaguar's engine idling and set the car in motion as soon as she was settled in her seat.

She glanced at him, feeling awkward, but he was looking at the road ahead, his expression impassive.

"Mom doesn't waste much time, does she?" she began tentatively.

He grimaced and shot her a quick look. "You realize that she won't stop until she thinks she's fixed our marital problems. We'd better get used to more of these cozy little outings."

"We don't have to. There's no reason we have to spend these outings together. You can drop me off in town," she announced triumphantly.

But instead of congratulating her on her brilliant plan, Reid gave her an impatient look. "Are you crazy? I can't leave you to wander around town by yourself all day."

"Why not?"

"At best you could kill a couple of hours checking out the museum and the shops, but that's it."

"So what? I'd find something to do to keep myself busy. I could go for a walk in the woods."

"No." He shook his head emphatically. "It's not a good idea to go off by yourself. It's a small town surrounded by miles of bush. You have no idea how quickly you could get lost out there. We'll stay together, but just do our own thing."

She sighed. "I guess you're right."

He glanced over at her, one eyebrow raised.

"What?"

"You just agreed with me, without arguing," he said in mock amazement.

She pulled a face at him, and he chuckled, an ordinary, amused sound. Here it was again, that unexpected moment of naturalness between them.

Determinedly, she steeled herself against the pleasure it gave her. She knew enough now not to read anything into it. "At least we don't have to put on an act when there's just the two of us."

"Now you're talking."

Who was she kidding? Hiding the effect of his presence on her all day would be far more demanding than the act she'd had to put on for her mother, or the whole village of Bancroft for that matter. With a nervous movement, she pulled a paperback out of her tote. She was counting on Noel Coward to be her refuge today.

"I brought a book and plan on spending the day reading. How about you?"

"Don't worry about me, I'll keep myself busy. You won't even know I'm around." He glanced over at her with a lazy smile that set her pulse fluttering.

She bit her lip and turned away to stare out the window into the leafy green woods. She'd have to be dead not to know he was around.

"Don't worry Joanna," he went on, "when we get back, at an appropriately late hour, we won't have any difficulty convincing Louise that we've spent a long relaxing day. Only *we* have to know that we spent it ignoring each other."

If only she *could* ignore him. It hurt to know that he found it so easy.

After driving a short distance along the highway, he turned off on to an unpaved road that followed the curve of a lake until they came to a small, deserted beach.

Reid frowned through the windshield. "There's usually at least a few people here, even this early in the season." He glanced at his watch. "Maybe it'll get busier later."

It didn't take a genius to figure out that he'd been hoping to find someone else here, so they wouldn't be all alone. He parked under the trees and Joanna got out to inspect the small arc of pale sand almost hidden by rustling birches and massive dark green hemlock.

While she was looking for a shady spot to spread her blanket, Reid unloaded things from the trunk of the car. He unfolded a lounge chair, settled himself comfortably and pulled a notebook computer from his briefcase. It looked as if he'd been true to his promise and had already forgotten she was there.

"I suppose this has been very inconvenient for you. With your work . . ." Why was she trying so hard to get his attention? Especially with such an inane comment. What about her resolve to keep out of his way?

"I'm the boss. I can do what I damn well want," he said lightly enough, but with that tone that told her only too clearly her intrusion wasn't welcome.

"I'm not prying, you know. I'm . . ." she trailed off. Of course she was prying! She stared at him helplessly. What did she want from him?

He settled the machine on his lap, flicked the switch and looked over at her with a bland, amiable expression. "These days, as long as I show up periodically, I don't have to be at the work sites all the time. But I will have to make at least one trip a week while we're up here. I have a few projects in the Kawarthas."

"Oh." She felt taken aback. He'd actually answered her question. For once he *wasn't* shutting her out. It emboldened her to pry some more. "What sort of projects are you working on?"

He gave her a long considering look. Just when she thought he wasn't going to answer, he said, "A few miles outside Peterborough, I'm building a rural retreat for a writer. It's completely self-sufficient—ground heat pump, solar panels." Enthusiasm lit his face and he became more animated. "You'd love the office—two stories high, bookcases from floor to ceiling and a library ladder. With a loft. We're using these beautiful cherrywood fixtures we salvaged from an old local church." He stopped abruptly, and the shutters came down again behind his innocuous smile. "But I'm sure that doesn't sound very exciting to you."

Joanna didn't need to be hit over the head one more time to get the picture. He simply didn't want to discuss his life with her; he didn't want to get that close.

"I'll get out of your way, then," she said stiffly. "I don't want to distract you."

"Oh, don't worry about that." He gave the brim of his straw hat a little flick and settled the computer more firmly on his lap. "I won't even know you're here."

"Good!" Joanna took a deep breath, trying to ignore the totally unreasonable stab of resentment. What was the matter with her? This was good, this was exactly what she'd planned. "I've got Noel Coward to keep me amused."

"I don't envy poor Noel," he said lightly. "That's a helluva job."

"Exactly what do you mean?" She smiled, but underneath she felt a little irked.

"Nothing much." He shrugged, but there was a smug curve to his mouth.

Damn! He was just *too* attractive, even when he was being irritating. "Come on, don't be obtuse."

"Well, it's just that *I* always had a tough time keeping you amused. Keeping you happy seemed to mean being at your constant beck and call."

"That's not true!" she protested, feeling the old frustration. He never had been able to understand what she needed from him. And talking about it always left her feeling that they were running on parallel lines, destined never to meet.

All she had wanted was a part of him. After their first six months together he had changed. The romantic, laidback man she'd married had vanished. Suddenly his work had consumed him, and making money was all that mattered. He'd insisted he was doing it for her, but she'd never asked for any of it.

Reid's smile faded and he gave her a long look. "It's amazing what time and distance can do to memory. The truth is, my dear, I couldn't satisfy you. Nothing I did made you happy." His tone was perfectly even, but she could see the small telltale pulse quivering beside his mouth. He wasn't as unaffected by this as he wanted her to think.

"Maybe because all I wanted from you was some time and it was the only thing you couldn't give me." She'd had no intention of getting into this, but she couldn't keep the old bitterness from coming through. "You had your priorities. I just happened to rate below your business. You always had plenty of time for that."

"My business!" Despite his careless laugh, she could tell that he was really annoyed now. "I worked my ass off so I could provide us with a good life. One that could compete with the support your father was so determined to give you."

The disparagement in his voice made her bristle. "My father only wanted to help. Why couldn't you accept that?"

"What kind of a man would I be if I let him support you while you were going to school? You were my wife. If anyone was going to support you, it was going to be me."

She exhaled sharply in exasperation. "I never understood why you made such a fuss about the money. It would have been mine anyway, eventually. Would you have had qualms about my taking it once he was dead?"

"You may find this hard to believe, Joanna, but yes, I would."

"So, in other words, just because you couldn't accept it, I couldn't either. It would have been nice if you could have asked me what *I* wanted...."

"That's right. That's what it always boils down to, what Joanna wants and to hell with the rest of the world." His eyes blazed with anger.

"Is that what you think of me?" A pained, humorless laugh escaped her.

Where did he get this idea of her? How could he have loved her if he thought she was like that? But then he hadn't loved her, it had just been a wild infatuation that faded when her needs got in the way of his ambition.

"No wonder you didn't lift a finger to stop me from leaving," she said bitterly. "You couldn't wait to wash your hands of me. I wasn't the wife you'd bargained for."

"You can say that again. But as for not lifting a finger to stop you, I tried to see you, remember? I sent you letters as well. You sent them back unopened."

"Letters?" She stared at him, uncomprehending. There hadn't been any letters! And if Reid had come, her father would have told her. Wouldn't he? The blood sang in her ears, and suddenly she felt sick.

"Don't tell me you never saw them." He shot her a cynical look. "I don't know why we're rehashing this stuff. It's all water under the bridge now."

The world rocked dizzily around her. She put a trembling hand to her forehead and felt numbness creeping through her. Her father had known how devastated she was by Reid's indifference. She could still remember him consoling her, telling her not to break her heart over a man who didn't even care enough to come after his wife.

Suddenly she couldn't breathe. Her father would never have done that to her. He'd never do something so hateful—he'd loved her!

She jumped to her feet and walked blindly across the warm pale sand, desperate to be alone, to try and assimilate this devastating revelation. She couldn't trust herself for one more second in front of Reid.

"Where are you going?"

"For a walk," she tossed back abruptly over her shoulder.

"I told you before, it's not a good idea to go walking in the woods by yourself."

"I think I can manage a little walk without getting into any trouble. I don't plan to go far." Ahead of her lay a narrow path that led into the trees, and privacy. If she could just hang on for a few more seconds, before giving in to the pain inside her.

"Make sure you stick to the trail!" Reid called out behind her, sounding a little concerned.

But as the trees closed around her she was aware of nothing but the frantic clamor of her own thoughts. Maybe Reid had only come once. Maybe that first day when she'd been so upset her father had thought it best to . . . But what about the letters?

She walked blindly along the path, hardly taking in the leafy-green quiet of the woods that surrounded her. No. There were no excuses. Her father had made all the decisions for her. *And she had let him*, she reminded herself harshly.

After all, she could have swallowed her pride and anger and gone back to Reid, tried to make him understand how unhappy she was. Instead she'd allowed her father to persuade her that Reid didn't love her, knowing that he'd never wholeheartedly approved of their marriage. And she'd eventually agreed that there was no point in remaining married to a man who didn't love her. That was certainly true now, but it might not have been true back then, if only she had been given the opportunity to find out.

Between herself and her father, any chance of reconciling with the one man who could have made her happy had been ruined. But what was the point of knowing all that now, when it was far too late?

REID STARED OUT at the glittering blue lake, feeling the knot of tension twisting painfully between his shoulder blades as he thought of the arrested look on Joanna's face.

Could it be that she *hadn't* known he'd come to see her? That the information had been kept from her? He wouldn't have put it past Jonathan to do something like that.

The computer landed on the ground with a thud as he jumped to his feet. He had to clear his mind right this second. He started for the lake, peeling off his shirt as he ran and plunged into the bracingly cold water headfirst. He came up gasping a few yards offshore, and gulped a lungful of air as he shivered and treaded water.

Okay, even if he gave her the benefit of the doubt, even if she knew nothing about his letters, or about his coming to see her, she still had to know about the divorce. Daddy's lawyer may have handled it, but Joanna had to sign the papers.

He struck out for a small island a few hundred feet away, pushing himself through the water with furious strokes.

After all, she hadn't called him, she hadn't written, she hadn't even come to get her things after the formalities were taken care of. Just one more way of rubbing in the fact that she wanted *nothing* that reminded her of him. Lady Bountiful, magnanimously letting him keep all the things they'd bought together. He'd ended up giving it all away to Goodwill. She wasn't the only one who'd wanted to start with a clean slate.

The rapid immersion in cold water followed by strenuous swimming had the muscles in his overtaxed arms and shoulders screaming with pain. He slowed his pace. Why was he letting himself get all steamed up about it again? It was over and done with.

He didn't want to be tormented with questions of why and what if. And Joanna's reappearance in his life had had one positive effect; it had stopped him from marrying again, for all the wrong reasons. One disastrous marriage was enough for any lifetime.

No, he wouldn't allow himself to get all wound up about Joanna. But he couldn't understand some of the things he felt provoked to say. Like last night, confronting her about wanting him. This lingering sexual spark made the situation difficult for both of them. Why had he spouted all that bunk about her craving a guy from the wrong side of the tracks?

He plunged his head into the cold lake, then lifted it up again, shaking the water from his eyes. It didn't matter, damn it. Because *she* didn't matter.

And there was no need to feel responsible for her. She'd made it very clear she could look after herself. Maybe he *should* have dropped her off in town today. Well, from now on that's exactly what he'd do. And she could do whatever the hell she wanted. He didn't care.

A piercing scream tore through the quiet and echoed off the distant cliffs.

Joanna!

His heart slammed against his ribs as he turned and struck out for the shore, the ferocious pounding in his chest making it hard to draw a breath.

He pictured the path she'd taken. It wound uphill to a small, wooded cliff. A fall from there . . . She could be lying unconscious somewhere.

Another terror-filled scream reached him as he splashed ashore. "Joanna!" he yelled, his voice hoarse with anxiety as he tore across the beach. "Honey, where are you? Can you hear me?"

"Reid, help me!"

Following the sound of her voice, he dashed into the woods, along the path that led inland, ignoring the sharp stones under his bare feet. "Hold on, I'm coming."

"Please, hurry!"

He ran along the narrow trail, desperately searching the undergrowth that made it impossible to see very far. His ears were filled with the pounding of his own heartbeat.

"Joanna, are you on the path?" he called out.

"Not exactly."

Rounding the corner, where the trail curved down to the water once more, he stopped dead in his tracks. There ahead of him stood a full-grown female moose, nibbling at the lower branches of an oak. Above her, just out of reach, Joanna straddled a branch, hanging on for dear life and watching the moose as if it were a ticking time bomb.

The staggering relief erupted from him in a roar of laughter that had him leaning his hands on his knees for support. She was safe!

The moose stopped eating and swung her massive head around toward him. Big, brown cowlike eyes regarded him steadily as the huge jaws kept up their ruminant chewing.

"What are you laughing at?" Joanna's indignant voice made him try manfully to sober up, but it was impossible. "Get me down from here!" she demanded.

The creature fixed him with a considering look, but gave no sign that it was about to leave.

"I'm sorry, I don't mean to laugh," he managed finally, even though that was a total lie. He felt giddy with relief. "You have to admit, though, this scene is just crying out for a camera. As a matter of fact if you can just hold that pose for a few minutes I'll run back and get the—"

"You'll do no such thing, Reid O'Connor!" she yelled furiously as he pretended to turn back along the path. He couldn't resist the opportunity to torment her just a little. After all, he'd almost busted a lung getting here. "Don't you dare go away and leave me alone with this . . . this—"

"Moose?" he suggested mildly, really beginning to enjoy himself now that the fright was over.

"—incredibly humongous animal." Narrowing her eyes, she shot him a killing look that only made him chuckle. "Get rid of it and get me down," she insisted. "You know how much I hate heights."

"Okay, okay. Calm down, relax. You know moose aren't aggressive animals, Joanna." He looked at the moose, which was still looking back at him and standing unnaturally still. "Come along, old girl. Let Joanna climb down out of that tree, although God alone knows how she got up there."

A sharp jab of pain stung the top of his head. He looked up just in time to see Joanna launching a second acorn in his direction. This one caught him square on the forehead.

"If you had a moose chasing you, you'd run, too." She still looked distinctly unamused.

He rubbed the stinging spot on his brow and gave her a taunting grin. "Joanna, everyone knows if you run from an animal it's going to chase you. If you had just stood still it would probably have passed you by."

"Are you going to stand there and lecture me, or are you going to get rid of the moose?"

"Spoilsport." He took a step forward and waved his arms. "Scat!"

The moose's answer was to lower her head and twitch her ears. Not a good sign.

Squaring his shoulders, he tried yelling. "Come on, get going!"

He clapped his hands, the sound echoing like a rifle shot in the quiet woods. But instead of running away, the animal lowered her head and began to move it from side to side as she started toward him, ears twitching and an aggressive gleam in her eyes. *Damn.*

"Reid, be careful," Joanna called out in alarm.

"Thanks for the advice."

He began to back away, but the moose broke into a trot that shook the ground under his feet. There was now only one thing any sensible person would do.

He turned and ran, aiming for a spreading marsh willow with one jutting branch barely within reach.

Close behind, he could hear the animal's pounding shuffle gaining on him. He could almost feel its breath on the back of his neck as he leapt for the branch. Pulling himself onto it in one muscle-wrenching motion, he winced as he scraped his bare chest and legs on the rough bark.

"Wow! Where did you learn to do that?" Joanna's sarcastic drawl reached him from the other tree. "I don't think I've ever seen such a graceful belly flop—outside of a swimming pool, that is."

"Ha, ha, very funny," he grunted, as he slowly and painfully hoisted himself upright on the branch.

"I'm surprised at you, Reid. Everyone knows you don't run from an animal," she mimicked mercilessly, then burst into a peal of laughter. Covering her face with her hands, she squealed helplessly. "Oh Lord, it was too funny.... You, running from that moose ... leaping into that tree ... oh, no ..."

He gave her a mock bow and said dryly, "By all means, laugh on. I'm so glad I've been able to take your mind off the fact that we're both stuck up a tree, with two thousand pounds of moose blocking our way down."

Reid seated himself firmly on the branch and leaned back against the trunk, looking as if he planned to be there for quite a while.

Dressed only in black shorts still damp from the water, he looked superbly fit and undeniably virile. When he'd jumped for the tree, his movements had been agile and strong. His body hadn't changed at all in the years since their divorce.

She felt a fresh stab of bitterness toward her father, followed by wrenching anguish. If only.... No, there was no point in tormenting herself with thoughts of what might have been. It was too late for that.

She shifted on the rough bark, trying to find a slightly less uncomfortable seat. "What are we going to do now?" she asked soberly.

Reid eyed her irritably from his perch across the clearing as the moose browsed a few inches below him. "How am I supposed to know?"

"What do you mean? You have to *do* something."

One corner of his mouth curved in sardonic amusement. "Like what? Do you have any suggestions?"

"No, but you're from around here, you should know—"

"Know what? I don't know how to break this to you, Joanna, but I haven't read the section in the woodsman's manual on getting rid of psychotic moose."

She looked down in alarm at the creature still placidly consuming the shrubbery below them. "So what are we going to do? Just sit here till it goes away?"

"That would be one school of thought."

"You're a big help."

He gave a negligent shrug. "I tried."

At that moment a loud crashing in the bush made Joanna look around in alarm. What now? All she needed was a bear to make the day complete.

Down below, emerging from the undergrowth, came two young moose calves on spindly legs. The female stopped browsing and headed for the lake. In awe, Joanna watched the ungainly little calves following their mother into the water to paddle along in her wake.

"Well, I'll be darned." Reid's soft voice brought her wondering gaze to his face.

A bemused smile curved his hard mouth as he watched the family swimming to the opposite shore. "She was keeping us safely out of the way till the young ones went by. I think it's perfectly safe to get down now."

As Joanna watched him climbing down from the tree, she too felt overcome by the wonder of the moment. But it was more than just the privilege of witnessing one of nature's small miracles. She had just remembered something, something that caused a tiny shiver of anticipation to ripple over her skin.

When Reid had come dashing to her rescue, she'd heard the fear and anxiety in his voice, before he found out that she was unharmed. Once again that seed of hope stirred inside her. Could it be that maybe, just maybe, he still cared a little for her? After all, he *had* come after her three years ago.

Already, he was climbing the tree and reaching up for her. "Here, give me your hand."

She leaned down toward him, a shy smile quivering on her lips. He responded with a sardonic twist to his mouth, but there was a look in his eyes she wanted to interpret as grudging kindness.

He reached the ground first and didn't step back as her feet touched solid earth. She turned to find him very close. Her senses swam with the heat of his body, the intoxicating smell of sun and fresh air on his bare flesh. A few drops of water still clung to his chest and she had to fight the longing to lean forward and lick those drops from his skin.

She was so breathless at how much she wanted him, she could hardly speak. "Thank you for coming to my rescue. It seems whenever I need you, you're there."

His mouth curved reluctantly. "You're welcome."

Emboldened by the smile, she felt a little reckless. "I guess you couldn't hate me all that much, after all."

His smile became wry. "No, I hate you, all right. But I wouldn't know what to say to Louise if I went home without you."

AFTER A LATE DINNER that evening, Joanna leaned back in a comfortable wooden lounge chair on the screened-in porch. The warm evening air, heavy with the scent of sun-baked pines, wafted over her as she looked out across the water, at the glassy rippling surface that threw back the glitter of stars and the shimmer of the low crescent moon.

From the radio softly playing in the background came music of the forties, which was eerily appropriate for a lazy summer evening in this timeless place.

At the first mellow strains of "Moonlight Serenade," her mother let out a nostalgic sigh. "Oh my . . . how your father and I used to love to dance." Sitting on the cushioned porch swing, she began rocking gently in time to the music. "Reid, dance with Joanna."

A little knot of tension tightened in Joanna's stomach. Since the moment he'd helped her down from the tree earlier in the afternoon, Reid had been distant, as if he regretted his softening toward her. And she had to remind herself not to take that softening too seriously either.

"Oh no, Mom," Joanna quickly tried to forestall her. "I'm exhausted from today."

"Goodness Joanna, what's the world coming to? A person can't go into a coma without finding that her child's turned into an old fuddy-duddy behind her back."

"Not old, just a fuddy-duddy." Reid's warm chuckle reached her from the dark corner where he sat, but it didn't fool her. He was acting again, and she was glad she couldn't see the indifference in his eyes.

"Joanna, have you forgotten how to have fun?"

Fun? After finding out about her father's betrayal? She was glad to be in shadow, knowing she couldn't hide the bitterness.

The only light came from the low lamp in the living room, which spilled out onto the porch, illuminating little more than the spot where Thelma sat knitting industriously. The rhythmic clicking of her needles blended with the ceaseless chirp of the crickets. The monotonous sounds were beginning to get on Joanna's nerves.

"Please, Mom. I'm tired."

"Tired! At your age I didn't know what it meant to be tired," her mother scoffed.

Had her mother always been so interfering? Or was it just the strain of pretending taking its toll? Either way, she didn't want to deal with this right now.

Reid got up and moved toward her. The soft lamplight outlined his broad shoulders and narrow hips, but didn't reach his face.

He stopped in front of her and held out his hand. "May I have this dance?" His voice was deep and husky with just a tinge of mockery.

Once again, he was doing a better job than she of playing his role. It was about time she learned to pretend as effectively, as cold-bloodedly as Reid.

Putting her hand in his, she felt his strong, calloused fingers close around hers, pulling her to her feet and into his arms. Arms that felt unyielding and unwelcoming, as cold and hard as stone.

Slowly, he began moving to the strains of the music, but his whole body radiated that shocking coldness. It formed an icy barrier between them that held her away from him.

A cloying, suffocating feeling enveloped her. She could stand his anger, she could stand his scorn, she could even take his ridicule, but she couldn't tolerate this cold, contemptuous indifference, made even more grotesque by the part he played so well—the role of a loving, attentive, caring husband.

Suddenly she couldn't bear being shut out. She had to break through that barrier. Without thinking, she pressed herself against him, then gasped as she felt her breasts yielding to his firm chest. He gave a small shudder, and a burst of excitement flared through her. She had made him react. And she was certainly reacting to him.

Closing her eyes, she allowed her body to flow softly against his hard strength. Once again she was aware of that trembling response and felt the frantic beating of his heart against her breast. Could this really be happening, this moment of just being so blissfully close to him once again? She felt almost frightened by the intensity of the feelings rushing through her.

To the languid strains of the music, Reid slowly danced her around the corner of the porch, out of sight of Thelma and her mother. Then abruptly, he pushed her away. Deprived of his warmth, her skin felt suddenly chilled and bereft.

Even in the dim light, she could see his chest rapidly rising and falling, as if he'd been running.

For one long, heart-stopping moment he searched her face, then his mouth twisted in a scornful smile. "Thanks for your generous invitation, but I think I'll do poor Paul a favor and decline."

His words hit her like a slap in the face. She flinched, mortified to the bone, and spun away, pushed blindly through the screen door and stumbled headlong down the wooden porch steps.

She headed for the lake and didn't stop until she reached the rocky slope at the water's edge where she sank down to her knees and pressed her hands to her burning cheeks. Had she lost her mind, along with her integrity? What about Paul? What about the woman Reid was engaged to?

Soft footfalls sounded on the smooth slope of rock behind her. She knew it was Reid without even turning around.

"Your mother wants you." His voice sounded low and harsh in the dark.

Getting to her feet, she took a deep, shuddering breath. She'd acted like a fool. It was time to pull together her tattered dignity.

"Thank you," she said, her voice subdued as she walked toward him, a dark, still shadow under the hemlocks. But as she passed by, his hand shot out and grabbed her arm, almost painfully.

"Don't mess around with me anymore, Joanna. I'm not here for your amusement and if you don't knock it off, you'll get more than you bargained for."

"Oh yeah, like what?" She lashed out at him in anger to cover her shame.

Suddenly he pulled her toward him and his lips came down on hers with a small, angry groan.

Her body went up in flames as he kissed her, his mouth hard and remorseless on hers. This was what she'd wanted, what she'd craved from that moment in her kitchen. To have him lose himself in his need for her.

She wanted to touch him back, but her hands were trapped between their bodies. As she tried to work them loose he stopped her by pulling her tightly against him and wrapping his arms around her. He deepened the kiss, plunging his tongue into her mouth. A flash of heat coursed through her, followed by the chilling realization that he didn't want her to touch him.

Frustrated and hurt, she worked her fingers into a position where she could grab a thin fold of skin on his chest and pinched, hard. Anything to pierce the formidable barrier protecting his emotions.

He flinched with the pain and grabbed her wrists, but his lips continued to move on hers, hard and unrelenting, yet still she could feel him holding back. Damn it, she was going to *make* him respond with a hunger to match her own.

She pressed her hips against him, then sucked in her breath as a slow liquid heat seeped between her legs, making her moan into his mouth. He was hard and straining against her belly. He did want her.

Abruptly he ended the kiss. His hands clamped her undulating hips, his fingers biting into her flesh to stop her movements. She could feel him shuddering violently. With an angry sound, he spun away.

Joanna stood mute and shaken by the raw emotions that had overtaken them, her mouth tingling from the wild storm of kisses. But like a fast-moving tide, a surge of empty, bitter defeat washed over her. It was still just sex. It had nothing to do with feelings.

What had she expected? She'd set out to get a reaction from him, and all because she couldn't bear the way he was shutting her out. Well, she'd got a reaction all right, but it hadn't given her any pleasure. If anything, it made her feel even more thoroughly ashamed of herself.

"Are you all right?" His voice throbbed with emotion as it reached her through the blessed darkness.

"Yes. I'm fine. Reid . . . I'm sorry . . ."

"Don't apologize." He expelled his breath sharply. "I must have been out of my mind. But from now on, please just stay away from me."

Then he turned and walked away into the night.

8

SUNDAY MORNING MISERY came creeping through the window with the cold gray light of dawn. Reid had already gone, or maybe he'd never come in. The sleeping bag was rolled up neatly and standing in the corner.

The bleak despair of the previous evening still filled Joanna. Sleep had changed nothing. How could she ever make amends for the way she had behaved?

With a sigh she threw back the duvet and got listlessly out of bed. She put on a robe, and headed for the cottage. Maybe a shower would help.

Utterly still in the early light, the lake looked ghostly. A fine mist drifted across the water, obscuring the opposite shore. There was no sign of Reid as she padded quietly into the silent cottage and headed for the bathroom.

When she emerged in shorts and a T-shirt, with a towel wrapped around her wet head, the smell of fresh coffee led her into the kitchen, where her mother and Thelma were moving about getting breakfast.

As she said good morning to them, she heard the screen door bang, and a moment later Reid stood in the kitchen doorway, looking remote and haggard. Where had he spent the night?

"Morning," he croaked to the room in general.

Avoiding her eyes, he smiled at the other two women, then turned and went toward the bathroom, his shoulders slumped beneath his navy T-shirt.

Joanna turned and found her mother watching her closely. Forcing a smile to her lips, she went over and gave her a hug and kiss.

"You're up early this morning." She tried her best to sound cheerful and normal, but wondered with a sinking heart what plans her mother had made for her and Reid today. Whatever they were, she'd have to find some excuse. After last night she just couldn't spend any time alone with him. "Did you sleep well?"

"I slept fine and I feel great. But you and Reid look like you should have spent more time in bed. You both look awful." Her mother gave her a shrewd, tight-lipped look before turning away to the coffeepot.

To cover her painful embarrassment, Joanna opened the refrigerator and took out a package of bacon and the box of eggs. When she turned around, her mother was standing in front of her with a mug of coffee in her hand.

"Here," she said, handing her the mug and relieving her of the eggs and bacon. "Take this to your husband. He looks as if he could use it."

No, not that! Utter panic shot through Joanna as she took the hot mug. "I . . . I'm sure he won't mind waiting till he comes out."

"Don't be silly, Joanna, the poor man looks like he hasn't slept at all." With a sly smile, and a roguish wink at Thelma, she said, "What have you been doing to him?"

Cradling the mug in her hands, Joanna hurried out of the room. It was impossible to hide her confusion. Better to face Reid; at least she didn't have to act with him. But that wasn't true, either. She was thoroughly trapped between a rock and a hard place.

She knocked on the bathroom door and listened for an answer, but could hear nothing except for the loud rush of the shower. Obviously he couldn't hear her over the sound of running water. So much the better. She'd just put the mug on the vanity and get out before he even knew she was there.

She opened the door and walked in just as Reid turned off the shower and swept the curtain aside.

Joanna stopped in her tracks and swallowed hard. He stood before her stark naked. Her eyes followed little rivulets of water that trickled slowly down over his chest and pooled in his navel. From there her stricken gaze was drawn irresistibly lower.

Her mouth went dry and her pulse accelerated at the achingly familiar sight of him. Suddenly he moved, and a towel covered his hips. She looked up to meet his hard, angry eyes.

"What do you want?"

"This is for you." Her hands shook as she put the mug of coffee on the counter beside the sink, then she turned and hurried out of the room. Her cheeks were burning, but even worse, she was acutely conscious of the throbbing ache between her thighs.

Her mother, seated at the table, looked up from buttering her toast and frowned. "Joanna, what's wrong?"

"Nothing!" She didn't mean her reply to be so sharp. Taking a deep breath, she made a conscious effort to calm herself.

A pan clattered in the kitchen as Thelma bustled about making breakfast, and the sound and smell of sizzling bacon filled the air. But it was all a meaningless buzz around Joanna as her mind rocked with the realization of how much her body craved Reid's. It wasn't getting easier to handle, it was getting worse.

"Are you sure?" Her mother's concerned look made her feel deeply uncomfortable.

"Of course." Joanna curved her lips in a smile that was meant to be carefree and reassuring, but she shuddered to think how unconvincing it must look.

Sure enough, the expression in her mother's eyes became grave. "Tell me honestly, this business with me is putting a strain on you two, isn't it? I'm just getting in the way."

"Don't be ridiculous," Joanna protested with a surge of panic. "You must know how much we love you, how important you are to us." At least she wasn't lying about that.

But her mother just shook her head, unconvinced. "There's something wrong between you and it worries me."

Remorse overwhelmed her. This was all her fault. She'd done a terrible job of holding up her end of the act. From this moment on, whatever it took, she had to make this work. She couldn't bear to see her mother fretting.

She bent down and gave her a tight, reassuring squeeze. "Don't worry about us, everything is fine. If we've been a little on edge it's because we've been so worried about *you*. We both love you very much."

Her mother looked up and a frown etched a line between the delicate blond brows. "I know that. But do you still love each other? Do you still love your husband, Joanna?"

The soft sweep of a door opening and a light footstep behind her told her of Reid's presence in the room.

"Of course I do." She forced a small laugh, as if that answer was the most natural in the world, but the irony of it filled her with aching despair. Reid thought she was only acting. She finally knew it was the simple truth.

It wasn't just sex she wanted from Reid. She still loved him, and she wanted him to love her back, but it was too late.

"How about you, Reid?" Her mother turned her piercing gaze to the man behind her. "Do you still love Joanna?"

"More and more each day."

Still stunned by her own realization, Joanna was dimly aware of how sincere he sounded. He was far better at acting than she was. But of course he had less complicated feelings to deal with—only dislike and indifference.

"Then why do you treat each other like poison? You hardly look at each other, you barely ever touch." Her mother's words snapped her back to reality. "Used to be you couldn't keep your hands off each other," she went on accusingly.

"Really, Mom, you don't expect us to act like new-lyweds, do you?" Joanna forced a teasing chuckle, but felt her stomach lurch.

"What I never expected was seeing you two going through the motions of a relationship, taking each other for granted. Where did all the passion go?"

Joanna opened her mouth, then closed it again. She couldn't bring herself to lie anymore. It was all she could do to stop the pain from showing.

Then she felt Reid's strong hands curling around her upper arms to pull her back against him. She leaned against the solid wall of his chest and could feel him trembling slightly.

"You're right Louise." Reid's voice was husky and confidential, just perfect for making an awkward confession. "We have fallen into a . . . rut. But we can climb out again, and will, so please don't worry about us."

He'd done his bit, and this was the point where she should turn into her husband's arms and sink into his embrace, confirm his optimistic words by her actions. But if he saw her face, he'd guess the truth. Instead Joanna crossed her arms, her chilled fingers covering his, warm and firm against her skin.

"Reid's right, Mom. We've just been working too hard and haven't been spending enough time with each other." Her voice sounded high and breathless, but it couldn't be helped.

It was difficult to return her mother's long, searching look. But it was better than facing Reid, so much easier to take than another dose of the cool indifference that was always there in his eyes, belying his words and smiles.

Just when she felt she couldn't stand another moment's scrutiny, a small smile touched her mother's lips. Whatever she saw in her, in Reid, satisfied her. "Well, from now on I'm going to see that the two of you have plenty of time with each other. I won't be happy until I see you cuddling and cooing again."

"I'm not sure about the cooing, but I think we could manage the cuddling." Reid's teasing voice and husky chuckle vibrated through his chest and into her back, until her whole body sang with his closeness and her legs weakened with desire.

God how she wanted to be held by him, the way he used to hold her—urgently, lovingly. But the hands curled around her arms were hard, and she could feel the tension in him. She could tell that he didn't want to be anywhere near her, much less holding her.

"The main thing is, you still love each other. So everything will be all right, won't it?"

All right? The tension around them was so palpable, you could cut it with a knife.

"That's where you're wrong." Thelma came in from the kitchen and put a plate of eggs on the table. "Love doesn't make everything all right."

"What do you mean, Thelma?" Her mother turned to her nurse with an inquiring smile. "If two people love each other, it can overcome anything."

The words pierced Joanna's numbing veil of misery. Had her mother always been this incredibly naive about love? But why not? Her own experience of it had been so perfect.

"Can it?" There was resigned cynicism in every line of Thelma's face, and she wasn't looking at her patient. Her uncomfortably penetrating black eyes gleamed as they focused on Joanna, then Reid.

"Well, of course it can!" With a gentle laugh her mother added complacently, "Love conquers all."

Thelma gave a mild snort. "It seems to me, the only thing it conquers is the poor fool suffering from it."

"Amen!" Reid's whisper made her realize he still stood behind her holding her arms. His warm breath made all the hairs on the back of her neck prickle.

She stepped away from him and darted a quick, alarmed glance at her mother, but she, thank heaven, was looking at Thelma, shock and pity mingled in her face.

"You couldn't feel that way if you'd ever *really* been in love." Her mother's voice was soft with sympathy, but rang with conviction.

To Joanna's surprise, a faraway, wistful look had crept into the nurse's dark eyes, softening her expression for a moment.

"Love can lead to trouble. Better to settle for contentment."

"But love makes you content because it brings happiness." Her mother sounded confused and worried.

"Does it?" Thelma looked directly at Joanna and raised an eyebrow.

Alarm bells went off. What had the woman guessed? That their marriage was in trouble, or that she did love her husband but it didn't bring her any happiness?

It was her mother who answered. "Of course it does. You've just let some bad experience embitter you toward the whole thing."

"Who's bitter?" Thelma shrugged and seated herself at the table. "I was married for twenty-five years, and they were good years. He was a good man, good to me, kind. He had integrity. That's something you don't find a lot of these days. I was never in love with him, but I liked him very much. We got on well, better than most."

"I'm glad." Her mother reached out to pat her nurse's hand. "Although I can't help feeling that it would have been better had you been in love, too. It may come with pain and suffering, but a true, strong love is worth it. It *is* better to have loved and lost, than never to have loved at all."

So quoth the woman who'd never experienced the down side of love, Joanna thought dryly. Her father had been the perfect husband—loving, attentive, faithful.

Joanna turned away to the window. Outside, the lake shimmered in the sun, but it all dissolved into a blur before her eyes.

Could she live without love? She would have to. Because there was only one man who stirred her blood, who could arouse a desire so acute that it cut her heart like a knife, but so blissful that she hungered for more. There was only one man who could make her feel anything, but he could also break her heart—and it wasn't Paul.

She glanced over at Thelma, who'd gone back into the kitchen and was just bringing another stack of toast to the table.

Thelma's attitude to life showed in her face, lined and old before her time. Ingrained cynicism shadowed her eyes and gave that downward curve to her mouth. In spite of her apparent contentment with her marriage, love had disappointed her.

Was that *her* future? Joanna wondered. It would be, if she didn't stop feeling sorry for herself and regretting the past. It wasn't Reid's fault that she still loved him, but he was lost to her. It was time she accepted it, really accepted it, and got on with her life. She could, and would, make Paul happy. She might not be "in love" with him, but she loved him, and that was probably a much more reliable emotion. And he *did* make her happy, she told herself forcefully.

MIDWAY THROUGH the morning Reid came back from town, where he'd escaped from the houseful of women right after breakfast. All that talk about love had made him edgy. As he climbed the porch steps with an armload of groceries, he was just in time to see Louise and Thelma heading off on their morning walk along the lakeside path.

In just two days the situation had become intolerable, and it was mostly due to that darling little woman and her tenacious efforts to fix a relationship. Only she had no idea how broken it really was.

He still shuddered at the thought of last night. What a total ass he'd made of himself. Joanna's behavior had been no mystery; like him, she'd reacted to the pressure they were both under, with her mother enthusiastically pushing them into each other's arms.

He strode into the cottage and stopped dead in his tracks. Joanna was standing on a chair in front of the fireplace wearing a pair of bright yellow rubber gloves, and fastidiously removing an old tea caddy from the mantel.

A yelp of laughter exploded from him. Who did she think she was kidding? Joanna, playing maid?

She turned wide, startled amber eyes in his direction. "What's so funny?"

"You look too precious for words."

"What do you mean?" She put her hands on her hips and glanced down at herself.

"Never mind, you wouldn't understand." His smile had faded, and he found his gaze lingering too long on the creamy-smooth skin of her bare shoulder. She was wearing a halter top tied low on her back and pale-colored shorts that hugged her rounded hips. There was no doubt about it, she was undeniably beautiful and lethally sexy. He didn't want to think about the way it had got the better of him last night. "Is this for real? You're cleaning?"

"These shelves need dusting. And I need something to do." She smiled, uncertain and a little self-conscious, and he hardened himself against the vulnerability in her face.

"You don't have to do that. I'll get someone in."

"I don't mind," she said quickly, then lowered her eyes to the old tin tea caddy in her hand. "Besides, it gives me a chance to examine this neat old stuff."

She'd changed. Instead of expecting someone to entertain and take care of her, she was finding ways to keep herself amused. Even pitching in and doing her share.

So what? Why was he getting all worked up? So she'd grown up. Everybody did, eventually.

"I'm sure you could find something more interesting than housework to keep you occupied. Peterborough's just over an hour away. There are shops and beauty salons and restaurants galore."

"Why do you persist in thinking that I'm so shallow?" Her eyes filled with hurt.

To his disgust, he found himself feeling guilty for putting it there. Why did he keep making her sound like someone she wasn't? He'd done it last night, too, had accused her of toying with him when he knew damn well that Joanna had never been casual or predatory about sex.

"I'll just get these groceries stowed away," he said gruffly, and walked into the kitchen feeling dissatisfied with himself. Why did he have to think about her at all? When it came to Joanna, he was one very confused man.

He stacked the canned goods in the cupboard, trying hard to ignore the sounds she made in the other room as she continued moving all the old junk from the mantel to the dining table. As he put the vegetables into the fridge he heard her gasp in surprise.

"Who is this man with you?"

He tensed, then forced himself to relax and shut the fridge door. Looked like there was no avoiding it now. He walked slowly into the living room and saw her standing by the fireplace, looking at a picture in its old and tarnished silver frame.

There he was at seventeen, standing beside Jack as they held up the huge muskie they'd finally managed to catch that long-ago summer. That had been the last time they'd been photographed together.

He swallowed hard, and wished like hell that he could turn back the clock. "My father."

"Your father!" Joanna gasped as she looked up at him, her eyes wide. "So this was your...your..." She faltered as she looked around her at the rustic cabin.

"Home. My humble beginnings." The words slipped out so easily now. There used to be a time he couldn't bear to talk about this place.

"But I thought you said this cottage belonged to a man named Jack? They named the lake after him. Your father's name was William. That's what you wrote on our marriage license...."

"His middle name was Jack. No one ever called him anything else."

"Why didn't you tell me this before?" She stared at him accusingly.

He gave a careless shrug. "I figured you'd kick up more of a fuss if you knew it was my place."

"I don't mean that!" She waved impatiently. "Why on earth didn't you tell me about your dad? Why didn't you tell me about this place when we were married? Why didn't you bring me up here?"

"I didn't think you'd be interested. I know I wasn't."

"Not interested! In your father? In your home? In *you?*"

"There was nothing to tell. Poverty isn't interesting."

Suddenly, understanding dawned on her face. "You were ashamed, weren't you? Ashamed of all this. Afraid I'd look down on you."

His voice hardened. "My father was an oddball, a loner, a man content to tap out rock samples and spend his life hidden away in the back of beyond. And yes, there was a time when I was ashamed to be the son of a man like him. It wasn't until it was too late that I finally came to appreciate the man my father had been. He didn't make the mistake of not being true to himself."

"But you didn't have enough faith in me to tell me all this when we were married." She sounded hurt.

He gave a humorless chuckle. "The ironic part is, it was myself I had no faith in." It had taken the breakup of his marriage to make him examine his own values and see that one of the reasons he'd failed was that he'd tried to be something he wasn't. "But why are we going over all this again? What does any of it have to do with the problems we're facing right now?"

"You're right. There's no use in dredging up the past. It's over." With a heavy sigh, Joanna put the picture down on the table and thoughtfully pulled off her rubber gloves.

What she'd just learned about his background might explain a lot of things, but it didn't change anything. And as for their current problems, she'd only managed to make them worse.

"Reid, about the...incident last night..." Her cheeks blazed red-hot, but she forced herself to go on. She wouldn't feel any better until she got this apology over and done with. "I promise you that'll never happen again."

He sighed and rubbed his eyes as if he was tired, then looked at her with a troubled frown. "This is a very difficult situation. We're being thrown at each other. I had no right to accuse you of the things I did."

The screen door opened with a screech as her mother and Thelma entered.

Reid started slightly at the noise, then said smoothly, "I'll see you later, honey. Don't wait up," as if he were ending a conversation, and turned away.

"Where are you going?"

For the first time Joanna blessed her mother's inquisitiveness.

"I've got a client in Peterborough, and I have to be there for the site survey."

"But it's Sunday!" her mother objected.

He shrugged and grabbed an apple from the fruit bowl on the table as he headed for the door. "Only day the client can make it."

"Joanna, why don't you go along?"

Her mother gave an encouraging nod, but Reid turned and shot her a meaningful look. The last thing he wanted was her company.

"Not this time." Hiding her dejection, Joanna waved to the table full of soiled and dusty objects. "I'm right in the middle of all this cleaning."

"I'll see you later," Reid said over his shoulder as he made his escape, but she caught his look of relief before he disappeared.

Her mother began to chuckle, drawing her attention back from the screen door as it banged shut behind him.

"What are you laughing at?" She didn't really care. Now that Reid was gone, everything seemed a little flat.

"The sight of you, doing housework." Shaking her head, her mother gave another chuckle. "How things change."

Joanna groaned and went back to the dusting that had suddenly lost its appeal. How could she cope with two more months of this? Pain when she was with Reid, ennui when he was gone. And the constant fear of exposing her feelings to him.

Heaven knows, she'd caused enough complications in Reid's life. The last thing he needed to know was that his ex-wife was still in love with him.

9

THE DOOR CREAKED slightly on the old hinges and she rolled over to see Reid framed in the doorway, a gilded shadow against the moonlit night. Then he stepped over the threshold and shut the door behind him with a soft click.

"Where have you been? I was so worried." She sat up on the bed, blinking in the shaft of moonlight that slanted in through the window and dazzled her eyes.

A small, husky groan cut through the darkness, a tortured sound that made every inch of her flesh tingle.

Looking down, she saw that she was naked, saw that the silver light sculpted the curve of her bare breasts and slightly rounded belly, and cast a shadow on the dark triangle between her thighs where she burned with a wet, aching heat that only he could soothe.

Slowly she got to her knees on the futon, knowing that the moonlight revealed her to him completely. Through the still darkness came the sound of his sharp, indrawn breath, and she felt her nipples tighten with an excruciating tingle.

"Joanna, I can't do this anymore.... I can't go on...."

Neither could she. She wanted him, needed him, now.

"Come here."

Was that her voice, so self-possessed and command-ing, without even a trace of shyness? Perhaps the dark was giving her courage, perhaps the moonlight had made her crazy.

To her surprise he obeyed, and came slowly toward her. Perhaps she was hallucinating. She reached out and felt the cool metal of his belt buckle. Her fingers tight-ened around it and she pulled him closer, marveling that her hand didn't even tremble.

To her amazement, he submitted to her imperious ac-tion. Only a few inches away now, he stood with his hands hanging loosely at his sides, gazing down at her, his eyes gleaming in the dark.

Her mouth went dry as she began slowly, boldly, un-doing his belt. But her fingers felt thick and clumsy, as if she were underwater. Try as she might, she couldn't seem to shake the deadness that suddenly pervaded her limbs.

His hand came up and covered her fingers, stilling them with an electric touch that brought everything sharply into focus. Her numbed senses became exqui-sitely keen.

Her breath came in short gasps as he slowly sank to his knees in front of her, his face only inches away from her aching, swollen breasts.

"Touch me . . . please touch me," she gasped out, de-sire making her voice thick.

He raised his hands and once again it seemed that ev-erything was happening in slow motion. She wanted to scream in frustration. Then his long fingers were cupping her breasts, molding them, twirling the nipples gently between his fingertips.

A shudder tore through her and she arched her back, thrusting her breasts against his hands. Her head felt too heavy on her neck and she allowed it to fall back.

Immediately his mouth was on her throat, his teeth biting gently into the soft flesh, kissing, sliding, warm and wet, down over the curve of her breast as his hands slipped under her arms. He lowered her to the mattress, his lips circled one aching nipple and he began to suckle with a hard, relentless rhythm.

With a shuddering moan, she writhed against his mouth as hot, swirling waves of arousal surged through her. The throbbing ache between her thighs intensified beyond bearing, the waves cresting to hang in tantalizing suspension.

Close, so close. On the brink, but somehow the ultimate release eluded her. Why wouldn't he touch her with the rest of his body? She wanted to feel him, on top of her, around her, inside her. . . .

A sharp, insistent knocking penetrated the sensual fog surrounding her. With a start, she woke to the sound of her mother's voice.

"Joanna, are you up?"

She jerked upright in bed and shoved the damp hair off her face. Her nightshirt clung to her hot, sweaty skin, and she was trembling all over.

"Yes, Mom . . . what is it?" She could barely get the words out. Her heart pounded frantically in her chest, and every inch of her body was flushed and throbbing with unsatisfied hunger.

"Can I come in? I need to talk to you."

Her heart went from beating too fast to not beating at all. Every vestige of frustrated desire vanished in an instant, and panic took over.

She heard her mother's hand on the doorknob, and saw it begin to turn. Wildly, she looked around and gasped in relief to see Reid in the sleeping bag, his tousled head just visible.

She had no idea when he'd come in, or who he'd been with. Business meetings didn't last past one in the morning, the last time she'd seen the clock before sleep overtook her. But his nocturnal wanderings weren't important anymore, and her relief at having him back, safe and sound, was short-lived. Her mother was going to walk in any moment.

Without giving herself time to think, Joanna scrambled off the futon and squirmed into the sleeping bag beside him.

"Sure, Mom, come on in." Her voice cracked, and breathing became an overwhelming challenge. Her heart began racing out of control again as she slid her body along the sleep-warm length of his, the motion pushing up her long shirt until it bunched around her waist and left the lower half of her body bare against him.

The door opened, and her mother's blond head appeared around the corner, her face wreathed in her usual ready smile.

"I'm sorry, I didn't mean to wake you up so early. . . ." Her voice tapered off, but a mischievous sparkle lit her eyes as she caught sight of them in the sleeping bag.

"It's not what you think," Joanna whispered hurriedly, hot with embarrassment. Any moment now Reid would wake up. What was *he* going to think?

Her irrepressible and incredibly annoying parent only lifted an eyebrow and said drolly, "Acting out fantasies is a very good way of keeping sex exciting. Your father and I did it all the time, but on the floor, Joanna? When there's a perfectly comfortable bed right there . . ." She chuckled and shook her head.

"Shh . . . not so loud," Joanna said in a hoarse whisper, anxiously scanning Reid's face for signs that he was awake.

Beside her in the sleeping bag, he shifted and turned toward her. Joanna froze, barely breathing, while he settled himself comfortably against her. One hair-roughened leg imprisoned her bare thighs and his groin pressed into her hip. Her mouth went dry.

"Sorry," her mother whispered back, with a finger against her lips, but she didn't look at all sorry. A teasing twinkle filled her green eyes.

But what did it matter what she thought of their sex life? Any moment now . . .

Too late. Reid's blurry gray eyes blinked open and focused on her face with a drowsy sensuality that made it impossible to look away.

He was pressed up against her. He felt so warm, a soft but substantial bulge contained by his cotton briefs. She remembered him *so* well. She could tell the very instant he became aware of how close they were. His eyes darkened, a hungry gleam in their depths that sent a shivery sensation swirling through the pit of her stomach. Then his body tensed, a dull flush spread along his cheekbones and his mouth tightened into a grim line.

Anger blazed in his eyes, and she felt him quivering with it, all along the length of her, felt the tension oozing out of every pore. Then she felt him growing hard against her thigh, and suddenly understood what he was so angry about.

"Good morning, Reid." Her mother's bright, cheerful voice sounded painfully incongruous.

"Morning, Louise." He raised himself on one elbow, rubbing the sleep out of his eyes with the other hand, the picture of groggy confusion.

"I'm sorry I woke you kids up." She didn't sound the least bit contrite.

"That's all right, I didn't want to spend the whole day in bed." His throaty chuckle was as deceiving as the intimacy in which they were apparently joined.

In actual fact, he was straining away from her, as far away as the cramped sleeping bag allowed. She knew he daren't get up and expose himself right now. He was her captive.

"I think that's exactly what the two of you should do. A long lazy morning in bed would be relaxing and—" a sly grin spread across her mother's face "—and very therapeutic. And there won't be anybody here to disturb you."

"What do you mean?" Joanna asked distractedly.

Right now, all she could think about was making love with Reid, and all that mattered was that he wanted her, as much as she wanted him.

Without conscious thought, she turned slightly and closed the minute gap between them. His chest molded to her back. With a tiny wriggle, she pressed her bare bottom against his erection. She felt him stir against her as a shudder went through his body. Oh yes, he definitely wanted her.

"Thelma and I are going into Peterborough for the day," her mother said lightly. "Is there anything you want, anything you need?"

"No, nothing," Joanna managed to reply, but her voice cracked.

"Liar." Reid's whisper feathered along her cheek, so softly that only she could hear it.

"Are you sure, dear?"

"Yes." The hoarse reply emerged automatically.

Of one thing she was very sure. She wanted him to take her right now. It could be done so easily, so quickly. Her thighs were parted and he was nestled, hot and hard, between them. She squeezed her thighs around him and heard his tiny gasp.

"In that case, can we borrow the Porsche?"

Every inch of her burned now, radiating heat. He must know, he must feel it. Turning her head a little, her startled gaze flew to his. Pure devilment lit up his eyes as he smiled down at her, a smile so potent she had to look away.

"Sure," she murmured absently as his hand stole around her waist, pulling her more firmly against him.

"Oh good. I told Thelma you wouldn't have a problem with that." Her mother eyed them with a complacent smirk.

In the dim recesses of her mind, Joanna knew that ordinarily she wouldn't dream of lending her temperamental, high-powered car to anyone. But right now she wasn't thinking about her car. She was just concentrating on the effort it took to breathe.

"And I'm sure Thelma's quite proficient with a stick shift," her mother went on, "although she admits it's been a while."

Her car, her mother's safety, her lack of judgment and responsibility, none of it mattered right now. All Joanna could think about was the small, but devastating movements of Reid's hips against hers, the rounded head of his shaft straining against the covering of soft cotton, her own aching need to feel him pushing into her throbbing heat. And all so controlled that the outer fabric of the sleeping bag betrayed nothing.

Her mother obviously didn't notice, but Joanna could feel her face glowing, every part of her trembling. It had been so long since they'd been like this.

Once again her mother's voice intruded. "I suppose it's like riding a bicycle, once you learn you never forget...."

Joanna gave a small start, until she remembered that her mother was talking about driving.

"No, never..." She hardly knew what she said; she hardly cared.

"Then I'll say toodles. Now don't wait up for us, we may be late." With a smug smile, her mother turned and left, shutting the door behind her.

"Toodles," Joanna replied breathlessly. But her mother was already gone and silence reigned, except for the sound of Reid's rapid breathing mingled with hers.

She should have said *Take me with you, save me from myself*. She should get up and get away from him, but she couldn't.

Slowly, she turned her head and looked up into the naked hunger that filled his eyes. As if in slow motion, he bent his head toward her. She held her breath and waited. After all, she'd been waiting for this moment for such a long time.

When his lips came down on hers she sighed and opened her mouth to him. This was no dream, not this time. This was real.

What was the point in fighting it? What was the point in denying that she wanted this more than anything else in the whole world? And suddenly she knew she couldn't stand the frustration one moment longer.

His lips were soft and firm, moving gently on hers, but she didn't want him to be gentle or to go slowly. Her body was crying out for satisfaction and she wanted it now.

She turned fully toward him and laced her fingers through his hair to bring his mouth more firmly against hers. But he pulled her hands away, and pinned her wrists against the pillow on either side of her head. His mouth continued its slow, unhurried exploration of hers, as if he had all the time in the world.

She struggled to loose her hands, but his grip only tightened. The leisurely, inexorable stimulation of his mouth was making her squirm with frustration. She wanted more, needed to be touched more thoroughly.

She dragged her mouth away from his with a gasp. "Let go of my hands."

"No." He kissed her once more, his lips now hard and demanding. Boldly, he pushed his tongue into her mouth again and again.

Vibrating with breathless excitement, she kissed him back ferociously, and this time when she strained at the captivity, he let her go, to run his hands eagerly over her body. She arched against his caresses, against the erotic abrasion of his calloused palms on her skin.

Hungrily, she reached down and rubbed the length of him through his cotton briefs. She remembered what he liked so well.

"No. I'll come too soon." His groan of protest only inflamed her.

"So what? I'll make sure you come again," she said with a husky laugh.

With an agonized moan, he sucked in his breath against her mouth. Taking his bottom lip between her teeth, she bit down gently as she slid her hand down his flat stomach, beneath the band of his briefs, and curled her fingers around him.

He groaned and shuddered. "You're so bad for me, but I can't stop."

A thrill raced through her. *Yes*. She still had the power to make him crazy.

Moving down his body, she took one hard, brown nipple into her mouth and sucked fiercely as her hand stroked the length of his shaft. He gasped for breath and tensed, but for a few moments he let her continue, one hand entangled in her hair, slowly massaging her scalp. The intensity of his reaction aroused her as if he'd been doing it to her.

And then, abruptly, he wound his fingers around a fistful of hair and pulled away from her.

"Hey! I wasn't done yet." She couldn't endure being stopped; she just wanted to touch him.

"My turn." His voice sounded strangled and hard as he rolled over until she was under him.

He pushed the sleeping bag down with his foot, exposing her squirming body to his fevered scrutiny. For a moment he just looked at her, his hot gaze slowly devouring her.

"What are you waiting for?" The tight voice didn't sound like her own.

He smiled grimly. "What's your hurry?"

She wanted to scream with frustration. But instead she lay still as he pulled off her nightshirt, then slowly lowered his head to take one aching nipple into his mouth. A long shuddering sigh escaped her as he ravished the peak with his hot, wet tongue, then moved his attention to her other breast.

The rasp of his beard stubble against her sensitized skin felt deliciously painful. She arched her back, wanting more, wanting it harder. Bending her leg, she rubbed her thigh against his erection and felt his pained indrawn breath against her breast.

He moved down her body, his mouth hot and wet on her belly, until he found the burning softness between her thighs. Hungrily, almost greedily, his mouth covered her. "...taste so good...so sweet," he murmured disjointedly against her, his tongue creating unbearable fire.

She was going to explode, but not like this! She wanted him inside her. Clenching her thighs together, she rolled away from his insistent mouth, at the same time pulling on his hair to bring him up to her.

"Not yet," he sighed, and tried to part her thighs with his hands.

"Please," she insisted.

With a groan of pure frustration, he moved up to capture her mouth with his. At the same moment she felt him slide into her, burying himself to the hilt. Even though she was ready and desperately wanting, when he entered her she gasped and bit down hard on her bottom lip, as he filled her almost to the point of pain.

Reid paused, breathing hard and leaned his forehead against hers.

"I'm sorry." His voice was shaky, his body trembling. "Did I hurt you?"

She shook her head, not trusting herself to speak for fear of bursting into tears. She'd missed him so much. He was the only man she had ever been, or would ever be, so desperately in love with.

"Joanna, are you all right?"

"Yes . . . please don't stop now," she pleaded breathlessly.

"I couldn't if I tried."

She could hear something harsh in his voice, almost like self-condemnation.

What did she expect? He didn't want this; he just couldn't help himself, either. This wasn't love, it was lust, but she'd take it. When it came to Reid she had no pride. She'd take whatever he was willing to give, and she'd give whatever he wanted to take. What did it matter? She was all his anyway.

And then he began to move, sliding in and out of her. Slowly at first, then faster, harder, deeper. Her hips were slammed into the floorboards, so hard and unforgiving beneath the sleeping bag, but she didn't care. She was making love with Reid again, and that was all that mattered.

Wrapping her arms around him, she met his thrusts with a fierce hunger she never knew she possessed. The heat of him, his weight against her breasts and belly, his musky male scent felt so familiar, so right, so satisfying.

Then he tensed and shuddered, and she felt him begin to come. Clenching her muscles around him, squeezing out every ounce of his hot fluid, her own orgasm exploded inside her, in quivering, pulsating waves of euphoria.

Reid held her tightly in his arms as she trembled, helpless under the onslaught. Still he continued to move, until she was gasping for him to stop, her nether lips so sensitive she could hardly bear the friction any longer.

But when he tried to pull out she closed herself around him and held him there. She couldn't bear to lose him, not yet. Too tired to protest, he collapsed onto her and lay still.

From outside came the fluting calls of the birds, and the soft, endless lapping of the water on the shore. But inside the cabin the only sound that broke the silence was the soft rasp of rapid breathing slowly being brought under control. She could stay like this forever, with Reid still inside her, filling her, making her want him again.

Reid felt himself stir and grow hard, even as the waves of physical release still trembled through his body. Despair washed over him. When it came to Joanna, satisfaction was out of reach.

But even knowing that, he couldn't help the desire flaring again as he slowly began to nibble gently at the delicate flesh of her throat where his lips rested. Even through the thin film of sweat, he could smell the faint fragrance of her lilac soap.

The scent of her turned him on, but so did the sight and sound of her. Everything about her spoke powerfully to his body. He was hard and aching again, and the only way to get any relief was to stroke himself inside her silken sheath. Slowly, so slowly. He didn't want to rush it . . . wanted to enjoy every moment of the heady friction, the heat . . .

"Hello, is anybody here?"

The distant but clear shout made him freeze. He felt Joanna stiffen beneath him, her muscles clenching painfully around his engorged flesh.

"What was that?" His gasp held a wealth of frustration. This was a hell of a time to be interrupted.

Her whole body arched, strung taut like a bowstring. Then she pushed at him frantically, her hands against his chest, her muscles clenching as she tried to push him out.

"It's Paul." Her stricken voice was a guilty sob.

He rolled off her as if she were made of hot coals and sprang to his feet. Shaking, he glared down at her through a red haze of anger as she clutched desperately at the sleeping bag to cover herself.

He grabbed his jeans and yanked them on, not daring to look at her anymore.

"I suggest you get dressed." He heard his own harsh, unforgiving voice echo in the small cabin. "Unless you want me to send him in to you and you can say hello properly?"

She flinched as if he'd slapped her. "How can you be so cruel?"

"Forgive me. I didn't realize I was being cruel. He *is* the man you love, the man you're going to marry, or had you forgotten?"

Her expression became cool and hard. "It seems we're both guilty of forgetting that."

He felt a stab of remorse. This was definitely not the time to tell her the truth about his engagement. Or the time to vent his anger over this messed-up situation.

"If I were you, I'd get rid of him before your mother gets home tonight. We don't need any more complications."

She bit her lip, her face tight with anxiety. "Reid, I..."

"I'll go put on some coffee and keep him entertained until you're ready." He didn't want to hear her glib excuses and explanations, or even worse, an apology. That would only be adding insult to injury. "But please hurry, this whole situation is a little too sophisticated for me."

He opened the door and stepped out into the clean, fresh air, leaving her alone to repair the ravages of his lovemaking, to wipe every trace of him away before she faced her fiancé.

10

A QUARTER OF AN HOUR later, Joanna stepped out of the cabin into the mid-morning sun. The mellow sound of music came drifting up on the warm breeze from the direction of the boathouse, The Platters singing "Twilight Time."

On any other day she would have found the song pleasantly soothing. Not now. The only thing she'd find soothing right now would be unconsciousness.

Had it been only three days since she'd driven up here? It felt like the longest three days of her life. Three days that had turned her world irrevocably upside down.

She took the path that led toward the water, and soon, through the trees, she could see Reid and Paul sitting on the weathered old dock that stretched from the boathouse out into the lake.

Reid had brought out a carafe of coffee, which sat on the small wrought-iron table between the two canvas deck chairs. Paul was sitting with his back to her, sipping from a steaming mug. There didn't seem to be much conversation, although both men appeared quite at ease as they sat listening to the music.

Screened by the trees, she paused for a moment to watch them. As usual, Paul was dressed with expensive elegance in cream linen trousers and a white polo shirt.

He looked refined, polished and very out of place in the rustic surroundings.

Reid, however, looked tough and uncompromisingly masculine in faded blue jeans that hugged his hips and long legs, and an old T-shirt that stretched across his broad shoulders and sculpted chest. His feet were bare and he looked relaxed and very much at home.

A blue jay darted overhead, startling her. All she needed was to be caught lurking among the trees, but the knowledge that she had to go down there and face them both, completely overwhelmed her. All she wanted to do was go away and hide.

With a sigh, she moved out from under the cover of the pines and walked down the side of the small frame building.

Paul turned at the sound of her footsteps and a warm smile lit his face. Unable to feel anything, she moved automatically toward him. He stood up eagerly and came to her, his hands stretched out to receive hers.

"Hello, my love." And then he was kissing her, his lips warm and clinging, the scent of his expensive cologne enveloping her.

Finally he pulled away and smiled into her eyes, sending her a fervent message that broke through her robotic detachment, filling her with pain.

"As you see, I couldn't stay away. The weekend felt like a lifetime. I missed you."

This was unbearable. She couldn't let it go on a moment longer. She'd hurt him enough, and he didn't even know it yet. Once she'd truly believed that she could make Paul happy, but he deserved a woman who loved him wholeheartedly.

"Paul, let's take a walk, I need to talk to you."

"Of course."

Something patient and resigned in his eyes made her wonder if he'd already guessed what she was going to tell him. Paul was no fool. Had he sensed something?

Steeling herself, she turned to Reid for the first time and saw only shuttered boredom on his face. "Would you please excuse us?"

"Hey, don't mind me," he drawled. "I'm just going to lie here and make up for lost sleep."

His indifference cut her to the core. As she walked away with Paul, another song came from the boathouse and echoed out across the water, the haunting voices of The Platters singing, "Only You". . . .

Suddenly tears blurred her vision and she stumbled. Paul reached out from behind and grabbed her around the hips to steady her. Holding her there, his fingers slowly massaged the curve of her flesh beneath her denim shorts. He took a step closer.

"Are you all right, Joanna?" he asked gently, his voice filled with concern, but she could also hear the resignation very clearly now. Paul knew. Dear God, he *knew*.

She shook her head as slow, hot tears burned her cheeks. "No . . . everything is just awful. . . ." She began to sob as the horror of it all came crashing in on her.

Paul turned her around, pulled her close and wrapped his arms around her. He held her, soothing her with soft words, stroking her hair, cradling her head while she wept with her face against his chest. The storm raged on until finally she was reduced to a few hiccuping sobs.

She lifted her head a fraction to see that the front of his beautiful soft white shirt was soaked, then sank her wet face against him again.

Gently, he stroked the damp strands of hair off her forehead. "It's love, isn't it?" His voice was deep and she could feel the vibrations against her cheek.

Relieved to finally admit it, she nodded her head against his chest. "Yes." Slowly, she raised her face to look up at him. It broke her heart to see the kindness and understanding in his dark eyes. "I'm sorry, Paul. I never meant this to happen, it just did."

"You don't have to explain it to me, Joanna. To be honest, I saw the writing on the wall the first time I watched the two of you together."

She felt a stab of remorse and took his hand, absently caressing his fingers. "I tried so hard to fight it," she said, more miserable now than ever.

"I know," he said consolingly, "but these things can't always be controlled, Joanna. I saw that you were different around him."

She groaned, feeling even worse.

"What's the matter?"

"Oh, nothing much." She gave him a sick smile. "It's bad enough that I have to feel the way I do about Reid, but to be so transparent..." A shudder went through her. If Paul had seen it, then how much more obvious must it have been to Reid?

"I don't think he noticed." Paul seemed to read her mind. "He was too busy hiding his own feelings."

Yeah, and she knew what those were, and they had nothing to do with love. "That's beside the point. I should have been more honest with you from the beginning."

"Joanna . . ." He put a finger under her chin and raised it until she met his serious eyes. "That evening at the gallery, I knew there was a risk that something like this could happen. So you see, you shouldn't feel so guilty. You weren't really doing anything behind my back." His lips curved in a wry smile.

She shook her head. "Don't be so kind to me. I don't deserve to be let off the hook. Let me feel how badly I've behaved toward you."

Capturing her hands, he gave them a squeeze and looked at her earnestly. "Listen to me, Joanna." He paused for a moment as if collecting his thoughts. "In all the time I've known you, you never talked about Reid, or your marriage. That told me the scars went deep. And I was hoping that by the time we got married you would be able to confide in me about what had gone wrong. But when I saw you and Reid together, I knew there was still much there between you. It was not over. You'd never looked at me the way you looked at him."

"Oh, Paul."

There was sadness in his eyes, but he smiled and shrugged his shoulders. "*C'est la vie, non?*"

A long silence stretched between them as Paul's gaze slowly roamed her face. "Don't look so unhappy,

Joanna. You've bruised my heart, but you haven't broken it irreparably. I will survive."

She sniffed. "You're just trying to make me feel better."

He chuckled. "Of course I'm trying to make you feel better."

She smiled wanly, her lips still trembling. "You're very sweet. I wouldn't blame you for being angry and disgusted with me."

He gave her a grave look. "Don't get me wrong, I love you very much. Nothing would have made me happier than to be your husband, but I don't want to be someone you just *settle* for. I want more than just your affection. How could either of us be happy unless we felt an equal passion for each other?"

A lump rose in her throat again. He was being noble and making this very easy for her. "I don't deserve you."

"True."

His droll expression made her smile.

He brushed away a tear on her cheek with his thumb. "That's better. I don't like to see you so upset." For a long moment he stared at her face, his expression grave and a little worried. "I really hope that this time it works for you and Reid."

"No, there's no chance of that." She couldn't keep the bitterness out of her voice and her small laugh was completely devoid of humor. "I said *I* loved *him*, I didn't say he felt the same way about me."

"Are you sure?" Paul's eyes narrowed skeptically.

"Very sure. He loathes me," she said acerbically.

"Perhaps, but I doubt it."

She didn't. She knew Reid far better than Paul did.

"Well, I still hope it all works out." He looked deep into her eyes and she saw his concern for her. "Let me know."

She nodded. There were no more words to be said, except goodbye. A lump formed in her throat. She desperately needed his friendship, but she was *not* going to ask him if they could be just friends. It was best to let him go.

"Come, walk me to my car." He put an arm around her waist and they made their way back over the rocky path and up toward the cottage.

At his car he took her hands and smiled into her eyes.

"I guess this is goodbye," she said.

"No, just *au revoir.* Remember me if you need a friend."

"Ditto." Her voice was husky and choked with tears. "Oh, your ring . . ." She began to pull it off.

He stopped her, enclosing her left hand between his palms. "Keep it. It's your ring, not mine."

"I can't." She drew her hand away and took off the ring, then handed it to him.

With a rueful smile, he slipped the diamond solitaire into the breast pocket of his shirt. Then he leaned forward and pressed a small, gentle kiss on her lips, before getting into his Mercedes and driving away.

As she watched the sleek black car vanish around the bend of the narrow road, fresh tears blurred her vision.

There went one of the most decent people she'd ever met. She was going to miss him very much. She turned to go back to the cottage, and her heart caught in her throat.

At the top of the path that led down toward the sauna, Reid stood watching her from beneath the shade of the birches.

How long had he been standing there, his hands shoved into the pockets of his jeans? And now he was no longer wearing his T-shirt.

Involuntarily her gaze swept over the firmly molded contours of his tanned chest, with the sprinkling of dark hair over the small brown nipples, and lingered on his flat, hard stomach. At last, she lifted her eyes to his face.

The tiny smile on his lips only conveyed his contempt, as his eyes fixed on her, mercilessly probing. "Do you feel better, now that you've had a chance to confess your sins?" Turning sharply away from her, he headed for the cabin.

Bleak anger shredded his insides. He couldn't take this situation a moment longer, couldn't live with his own weakness. He hadn't been exactly roped and gagged in that sleeping bag this morning. He could have exercised his willpower. And he should have.

But this morning he'd forgotten everything. His self-respect, his common sense, his cardinal rule that other men's women were off-limits. He'd done to Paul what he could never stand being done to him, and that left a really bad taste in his mouth.

And what now? Were they going to continue as if nothing had happened? *No.* He couldn't take any more of this. He certainly couldn't take one more night sleeping in the same room with her.

FROM THE PICTURE window of the cottage Joanna watched Reid stalking grimly toward the sauna, his rolled sleeping bag under one arm and a hard, implacable look on his face.

With a groan, she closed her eyes and leaned her forehead against the cool glass of the window. She'd made such a mess of everything. Why couldn't she accept the reality?

Because she needed him, because she loved him. Because when she was in his arms she felt that she belonged. And she couldn't change those feelings no matter how hard she tried, and no matter how brutally Reid reminded her that he didn't share them.

It didn't take a rocket scientist to figure out that he was prepared to brave the discomforts of sleeping in a sauna rather than share a room with her.

She should feel relieved. After all, before Paul's arrival, hadn't she been stewing about how was she going to endure the rest of the time spent with Reid? Now all she could think of was how to stop herself from needing him.

She lifted her head from the glass, opened her eyes and blinked as a brilliant shaft of sunlight pierced a gap in the dark, fast-moving clouds.

Without stopping to think, she headed for the door. Why was she following him? Because Paul had planted a seed of hope. Was he right? Did Reid feel something too? But even if he did, what about the woman he planned to marry? She tried to ignore the selfish little voice reminding her that he wasn't married yet, that he was still fair game.

She ran lightly down the steps and crossed the smooth rock, spotted now with dark raindrops, all too aware that she was looking for trouble. And she'd have no one but herself to blame when she found it.

She paused in the doorway of the sauna, her body blocking the only light that could enter the square, windowless room. Reid was sweeping the cedar floorboards with an old straw broom, but as she stepped over the threshold he stopped and turned to face her.

His eyes glittered with wary suspicion. "What do you want?"

Outside a slow, steady drizzle had begun to fall. Inside the small room the atmosphere was thickened with silent tension and filled with the sound of the rain pattering on the sauna roof and splashing off the surface of the lake.

Joanna swallowed convulsively and licked her lips. "Paul and I aren't engaged anymore," she blurted out, as a wave of heat spread through her body. She knew her cheeks must be glowing scarlet.

That wasn't the first thing she'd meant to say. But then again, what words had she intended?

"Don't worry, I'm sure you'll bring him around. You can be very persuasive." His mouth quirked in a derisive smile and he turned back to his sweeping. "After all," he added lightly, "you usually get what you want, don't you?"

A cold wave of misery and anger descended on her. So he still thought of her as a selfish bitch. How could she have thought for even a moment that he really cared about her? Perhaps then, it was time she lived up to her reputation.

"I hope so," she said, deliberately hardening her voice, "because right now, I want you."

11

FOR A MOMENT Reid stood utterly still, his broom poised just above the floorboards. Then he turned slowly to face her, his eyes glittering with anger and frustration. A small shiver, part excitement, part apprehension, trembled low in her belly.

"Are you trying to prove something, Joanna?" He ground out the words between stiffened lips.

Feeling reckless and driven, her mouth curved in a smile that held no amusement. "I'm trying to prove you right. Aren't you glad?" Lifting her chin defiantly, she gave him an insolent look. "I *can* have anything I want, including you."

"If you mean you could entice me into having sex with you again, you're probably right." His eyes blazed a warning. "But you might not enjoy it quite as much this time."

"Now you're just being modest," she taunted.

In an instant, he struck. His hands curled around her upper arms to pull her roughly against his hard, trembling body.

For a brief moment she was actually afraid, afraid of the way his skin had suddenly paled, the pulse leaping beside his mouth, knowing she'd driven him beyond endurance. Hardly breathing, she stood as if turned to stone and stared into his face.

And then slowly the anger began to ebb from the storm-gray depths of his eyes and tired defeat crept in. The grip of his fingers loosened a little.

Damn! Her fear disappeared in a rush of frustration. She didn't want him to control himself, to simply give up. She wanted him to lose it. To lose himself in her.

Raising herself on tiptoe, she pressed her pelvis against his. He was hard and straining against his jeans. She rubbed herself against him, deliberately making her movements small, almost imperceptible. It worked.

His eyes darkened, a hectic slash of color stained his cheekbones and he drew her fiercely against him.

"You're an unfeeling bitch, do you know that, Joanna?" he muttered thickly.

Then his hungry lips were clinging to hers, and she opened her mouth wide to him. Her heart was beating out of control, almost suffocating her.

His mouth ravished her lips, her face, her throat as he backed her up against the wood-paneled wall. He tugged at her clothing, his fingers shaking as badly as her own hands that were fumbling with the button at the waistband of his jeans.

He yanked down her shorts and she stepped out of them. She frantically kicked them aside, and finally managed to undo the button she'd been struggling with and pull down his zipper.

With his hands under her buttocks, he lifted her and she wound her legs around his waist while he fought urgently to pull his jeans down and free himself.

Fastening his mouth once more on hers, he pushed into her. She gasped at the momentary discomfort, then clung to him as the length of him filled her, stretched her with a deep, hard, thrust, burying himself in her tight, wet sheath.

He'd never entered her so quickly, so ungently before, with no stroking and fondling to moisten his way. He was trying to punish her. Right now, however, she didn't care.

All that lazy indifference earlier, all his self-control and reluctance now—what a sham it had been. He wanted her as desperately as she wanted him.

With a moan, she dug her fingertips into the bunched muscles of his shoulders, sweat pouring from her body as he started to move. Slow, powerful strokes pushed her against the wall in an unrelenting rhythm. A rush of liquid heat, beyond anything she'd ever known before, pooled between her thighs.

Slowly she opened her eyes. Through a haze she found him watching her with a burning intensity, watching the play of emotions on her face as he slid forcefully in and out of her. His own face was flushed, his jaw clenched.

Suddenly he groaned, and his rhythm increased, his fingers digging into her hips almost painfully. Once again his mouth covered hers and his tongue plunged into her with ruthless determination, probing deeply, feverishly entwining with hers.

She kept her eyes open and saw that he did the same. She wanted to watch his face so that way she knew he was making love to *her*, not someone else. Right now she wanted to make him forget everything and everybody but her.

Her body burned even hotter as the soaring sensation spiraled closer and closer to the brink. She felt the edge of the euphoric frenzy she craved, and then she wasn't thinking any longer, as she trembled, teetering on the pinnacle of release.

A frantic moan tore from her throat as the orgasm hit her. She shivered and jerked against him, her muscles contracting wildly around his hot, hard shaft. A moment later she felt his sobbing series of convulsions as he came too, deep inside her. She clenched her muscles, but held still, her sodden T-shirt plastered against the rough wood wall.

Dimly, she became aware of the rain-laden breeze wafting in through the open door, of the soft liquid pattering outside, of muted birdcalls and the rustle of the trees. Every fiber of her being was excruciatingly attuned to Reid, the heaving of his warm chest against her breasts, the scent of soap and sweat on his glistening flesh. She pressed her lips against the bronze curve of his shoulder, then ran her tongue along his skin, savoring the salty tang.

She thrilled to feel him tremble and grind his hips against her a few more times, driving in as deep as he could get. Then all at once he slumped and began to pull himself out.

No, not yet! She tightened her muscles around him, but couldn't hold him as he slid away from her. Bereft and exhausted, she sagged against his chest.

She didn't want to move. It felt as if she'd expended every ounce of energy she possessed, and she doubted that she could even stand right now. Besides, she couldn't think of anything more wonderful than the feel of his body, warm and relaxed against hers.

More than anything else in the world she wanted him to hold her, but as if reading her thoughts, he stiffened. Reluctantly, she allowed him to lower her slowly to her feet, her body grazing against the rigid length of his.

She didn't want to look at his face; she could feel his anger only too keenly. But when he spoke she realized that fury was self-directed.

"I guess I've sunk about as low as I can." He stepped away and yanked his jeans up over his hips in one sharp, jerky movement. Then he reached down, picked up her shorts and held them out to her.

She had to look at him as she took the shorts from his hand. His face was a terrible, rigid mask. He held her gaze, but his eyes looked bleak and to her horror she saw that they were moist.

"I'm sorry," he said quietly. "I don't know what else to say...."

"There's no need for you to say anything. And there's no need to apologize." Her heart shattered into little pieces. She wanted to hold him, comfort him. "It was my fault."

"I as good as raped you."

"Hardly. You did nothing against my will."

"Joanna . . ."

"Please, Reid, don't say another word." The remorse in his eyes cut her to the bone. "You know as well as I do it was my fault. I pushed you into doing something you despise. I'm the one who should apologize."

"No one can make you do something you don't want to." His voice was low and hard. "I'm responsible for my own actions, and I'm ashamed of myself."

"Please, I don't want to talk about this anymore." Afraid of completely losing control in front of him, she rushed blindly past him and outside into the ebbing drizzle.

Why, why had she done such a stupid, selfish thing? Resentment—pure, mindless resentment. And all because Reid hadn't reacted the way she'd hoped to the news of her broken engagement. But what had she been expecting? That he'd beg her for another chance now that she was free? How naive of her, how pitiful. As if that were the only thing keeping them apart.

And her punishment for her selfish behavior was knowing that Reid condemned himself for his actions, knowing that she had to push him beyond the limit before he'd appease his frustration by taking her body. How low had she sunk?

Blindly, she ran across the wet rocks, tears coursing down her cheeks and mingling with the last spatters of rain. A bleak, hopeless feeling chilled her to the bone.

Life stretched out ahead, endless and empty. Reid wouldn't want her if she were the last available woman on earth. How could she have thought, even for a second, that he could care about her? That they might have another chance together?

The crunch of tires on wet gravel made her look up toward the cottage. The Porsche rounded the bend and pulled up—with a star-shaped hole, dead center in the windshield.

Every thought fled, pushed out of her head by a wave of fear. She dashed uphill over the slippery rock, reached the car and yanked open the passenger door.

"Mom, are you all right? What happened?"

"Now, before you get all bent out of shape, it wasn't Thelma's fault." Her mother testily pushed Joanna's hands away as she tried to help her out of the car. "Stop fussing, I can manage." She hauled herself out of her seat and brushed off her white linen slacks.

Joanna anxiously looked her over. She didn't *look* hurt.

"Thelma's been worried sick all the way back about what you'd say." Her mother fixed her with a determined stare. "Now I want you to promise to stay calm."

Joanna gritted her teeth. "Just tell me what happened."

"Well, it was like this," her mother began. "Thelma and I were in the bank, and just as I got up to the cashier, I heard a man yelling at us to get down on the floor. At first I couldn't understand what was happening. Then I realized that the bank was being held up. The men had guns and everything."

Joanna let out an involuntary gasp. "What! I can't believe this!"

"Well, it's true," Thelma added, as she emerged from the driver's side.

"They took all the money, then they ran out the door," her mother continued. "But just then, a whole slew of patrol cars pulled up, just like in the movies, and all sorts of policemen in bulletproof vests jumped out with their guns drawn. And then we heard some shots, but unfortunately we couldn't see anything." Her eyes were round and gleaming with excitement as she told the story. "Shortly after that we saw the two men handcuffed and led away to a police car. It was all very thrilling."

"Yeah, till we went back to the car." Thelma eyed the windshield in dismay. "One of the shots we heard got your Porsche—right between the eyes." She took out a folded pink sheet of paper from her purse and handed it to Joanna. "Here's a copy of the police report for your insurance company."

After a moment's hesitation, Thelma pulled out a yellow slip. "And, um, we got a ticket. We were in a No Parking zone."

"Now it wasn't your fault, Thelma, dear," her mother consoled her. "It was my idea to park there."

Her head reeling, Joanna took the pieces of paper and stuffed them into her shorts pocket. The whole day was like some kind of bad dream—from the moment her mother had walked in and forced her into that sleeping bag with Reid, to this. And what made it even more bizarre was the way her mother, instead of being shaken and upset, acted as if a violent crime had been entertainment put on for her benefit. Joanna was aware that Reid had come up from the sauna and was standing just behind her. After what she'd just done, she couldn't even look at him, and one thing was very clear to her. She had messed him up enough. She was going to tell her mother about the divorce. If she was strong enough to weather the shock she'd just experienced, then she was strong enough to hear the truth.

"Mom, let's go inside. We need to talk." It was amazing, really, how steady and calm she sounded, even dispassionate.

Her mother's expression sharpened and her shrewd eyes darted to Reid and rested on him for a long moment. Then slowly, the penetrating gaze turned to her. For the first time Joanna could meet it, and hold it, without any discomfort. After all, there was nothing left to hide now. Let her see it all.

Her mother solemnly turned away and moved toward the cottage, but not before Joanna saw the disappointment in her eyes.

She followed, acutely aware of Reid right behind her. Soon there'd be no reason for her to stay. But she knew with terrible certainty that no matter where she went, no matter what she did, there'd always be too many reminders of Reid.

Somehow her legs carried her around the building to the steps, and up the steps to the deck. She opened the screen door and walked through, then stopped in the middle of the room. Her veins seemed to run with ice.

From the corner of her eye she noticed that Reid had come in and remained standing by the door, his hands shoved in his pockets. He made no move to join them. She was thankful for that, at least. And Thelma had tactfully remained outside.

"Let's sit down." She walked over to the table by the window and waited for her mother to be seated before she sank down onto a chair. She laid her hands on her lap, laced her fingers together, sat up very straight and took a deep breath.

Looking up, she met her mother's gaze and received a painful jolt. There was a wealth of sadness shimmering in the beloved pale green eyes.

Joanna felt a stab of guilt. She was about to repay all that love and devotion by revealing the shameful deception she'd perpetrated. Reid had been right: this was going to hurt her mother far more than if she'd been honest all those weeks ago.

Unable to bear the unhappiness in her mother's face, Joanna shifted in her chair to look out the window. The scene outside was nothing but a blur of greens and blues.

"Mom, I've lied to you," she blurted out in a shaky voice. "Reid and I are not married anymore. We just pretended to be, because when you first woke up, I was afraid you weren't strong enough to hear the truth. I'm sorry I lied."

After her rush of words, the silence lengthened inside the room, broken only by the faint whine of a mosquito against the door screen and the distant sound of lapping water.

Joanna swallowed the painful lump in her throat, before turning her head to look at her mother, afraid of what she'd find.

But her mother didn't look shocked, or crushed. Her gently lined face had a look of calm resignation.

A small sigh escaped her. "And I'm sorry I pretended to believe you."

12

"PRETENDED?"

"I'm afraid so, dear." Her mother sounded so placid it was unreal.

"How long have you known?" Joanna's voice cracked and she brushed away a tear with an angry swipe.

"From the very beginning."

For a moment there was dead silence. Then Joanna swayed to her feet, knocking her chair over. Trembling in every limb, her voice emerged in shaky gasps. "All this time you knew...and you made us go through all this...this..." Words failed her. She covered her face with shaking hands.

When she looked up there was concern on her mother's face, but Joanna could feel no sympathy, only bitterness and utter humiliation.

"How could you? Why?" Throwing up her hands, she turned her head away. "No, don't tell me why, I don't want to know. It hardly matters anyway," she said wildly. Nothing mattered anymore. "The damage has already been done."

"Joanna, calm down. Let me explain."

"I don't want to hear any stupid explanations. And don't you tell me to calm down! I have a right to feel betrayed and angry."

Hot, burning tears were flowing freely down her cheeks now, but she didn't care. She was past caring.

"I'm going to explain anyway," her mother said calmly, her face composed, if a little pale. "I knew there was something wrong when I asked you about your ring," she said gently. "You looked so guilty, so stricken. Then I realized you weren't wearing your wedding band. But when I asked you about Reid, the look on your face . . ." She shook her head sadly. "I knew you weren't married to each other anymore."

Joanna felt the hysteria ebbing, but the bitterness remained. "So we've gone through all this pain and trouble for nothing. Did you ever stop to think how much harm you were doing to Reid, to me?"

"No. All I could think of was that I had to stop you from making a very big mistake. I couldn't let you marry someone else, not when I could see there was still something there between you and Reid, feelings that hadn't died."

Joanna's voice was cold and hard. "And I don't suppose it ever occurred to you that you were mistaken?"

"No," came the soft but definite answer. "I know the two of you and it was as plain as the nose on your face that there were feelings between you that hadn't been put to rest."

"Speaking for myself, the only thing I felt was mortified that I had to go to Reid and ask him for such an enormous favor." Only the anger hardening her voice made it possible to sound convincing. "But that's beside the point. Do you realize what you've done? You had no right to manipulate us like that."

"I have every right in the world, Joanna." Her mother got to her feet and looked up into her face. She was still thin and delicate-looking, but the steely glint in her eye betrayed the indomitable spirit that had brought her back from the brink of death. "I am your mother. I would be derelict in my duty if I didn't do something to prevent you from ruining your life."

"My life!" Joanna was aghast. "You knew nothing about my life—you'd been in a coma. I'd finally found what I was looking for...."

"I could see you were unhappy. And please don't bother denying it. You're my child. I know you better than you know yourself."

Joanna fell silent. How could she keep disputing the truth? But she couldn't let her mother expose her any further in front of Reid. She knew him. He'd feel badly for her; he'd feel responsible and to blame. He'd feel everything but the one thing she wanted him to feel for her. Love.

Carefully not looking in Reid's direction, she said evenly, "We'll talk about this later. Right now I want you and Thelma to pack your bags. We're going home."

"Joanna, no!" Her mother clutched her arm, digging her fingers in with surprising force. "Don't be a fool, don't throw it all away. Stay."

She put her hand over her mother's and massaged the thin fingers, trying to ease her grip. "It's too late, Mom, much too late."

The thin fingers tightened, and the green eyes became intensely pleading. "It's never too late if you love each other."

"That's a big if." With a herculean effort, Joanna kept her voice steady and drew her mother's hands into her own. She even managed a small, wry smile. All her anger had drained away, leaving her limp and tired.

"Are you trying to tell me you don't love your husband?"

"He's not my husband anymore. We're divorced, and he's engaged to another woman. That should give you your answer." Her glance slid away toward the window. She was incapable of looking at her mother and telling an outright lie.

"That's not an answer."

Joanna stepped back and let go of her mother's hands, conscious of the perceptiveness in her mother's quiet voice. "That's all the answer you're getting out of me. I know you have my best interests at heart, but I'd like you to mind your own business. I'm going to pack my stuff."

Stiffly, she turned to face Reid and her breath choked her. Inevitably, she'd have to see him again. He was bound to come and visit her mother. Would he bring his wife? How was she going to stand the pain?

Forcing a smile to her frozen lips, she held out her hand. He looked at it for a long moment, then reached out to take it in his, a somber expression on his face. At the touch of his fingers on her skin, as his familiar warmth and strength flowed into her, she felt tears springing into her eyes again. Ruthlessly, she blinked them back. She was going to hang tough if it killed her.

"Thanks for all you've done. I know it hasn't been easy. I'm sorry about everything." The words came automatically. She was hardly aware of what she said.

His brow creased, the grave look deepened. "Joanna..."

She drew back a little and held up a hand. "No, please, Reid, don't say anything. This whole mess is my fault, I should have listened to you. But you helped me anyway, and you went beyond the call of duty to do it. I just want to thank you and wish you all the best...." Her heart rose up in her throat and she couldn't go on.

She turned quickly away and rushed headlong out of the cottage.

THE SHADOWS OF the marble columns were lengthening across the lawn as Joanna drove up to the house. The long day at the gallery had left her exhausted.

It was her first day back, after the weekend away that had seemed more like a lifetime, and she'd walked into another episode in this nightmare that her life had become.

Some club patron had lost control of his car in the early hours of the morning and crashed straight through her plate-glass window. No paintings had been damaged, thank goodness, but the place was a shambles. Coping with the aftermath had been a marathon of cleaning up the mess of glass, having the window replaced and dealing with the insurance people.

But now she was home at last. After putting the car in the garage, she paused to look out over the bluffs at the blue expanse of Lake Ontario, so serene and unruffled. If only the beautiful view could calm her troubled soul. All day she'd been depressed and distracted, unable to stop thinking about Reid. Was he back in the city yet?

After running headlong from the cottage the day before, she'd packed and been ready to leave within the hour, only to find that her mother and Thelma intended to stay on for the rest of the summer. Reid had offered to arrange for a rental car and cellular phone before he too came back to Toronto.

This time she hadn't argued with him about his officiousness. All she'd wanted to do was get home. After an hour's delay having her windshield replaced in Bancroft, she'd spent another miserable three hours driving back, crying most of the way.

She fitted her key in the lock. She was home, but there was no relief here, no comfort. The emptiness inside her was there to stay. Without Reid, part of her would always be missing. But life did go on, and hers would, too. Eventually she'd get used to the emptiness and it wouldn't hurt so much.

As she walked through the door, the phone began to ring. At the same instant, Halton appeared in the foyer, tall, gray-haired and smiling in welcome, just as always.

"Good evening, miss." Efficiently, he relieved her of her briefcase and jacket.

"Good evening, Halton." Her own smile was tired and a little forced as she headed for the living room. "Don't worry, I'll get it."

It could be her mother trying out her new phone. It could be Reid. Her heart fluttered madly against her ribs as she crossed the room. No, he wouldn't call.

Her hand shaking slightly, she picked up the receiver. "Hello."

"Hello. Joanna, is that you?" The loud impatient voice hurt her ear. She sighed and held the phone away from her head a little as she sank down onto the sofa in front of the fireplace.

"Yes, it's me, Alexei."

Twenty minutes later she wearily set down the phone, after having convinced Alexei that his paintings were completely safe, and that a freak accident like that wasn't bad karma.

Feeling wrung out and depressed to the bone, she rested her head on the back of the sofa and shut her eyes. When she opened them she saw Halton standing in the doorway, gravely watching her.

"I don't want to talk to anyone or see anyone this evening. I want to be left alone. Unless it's my mother, of course," she added reluctantly.

She got to her feet and headed for the hallway. "I'm going to take a shower now," she told the butler as she passed him, "but I'd like a tray in the living room when I'm done. Nothing major, just a sandwich maybe or a bowl of soup. Thanks, Halton."

At the bottom of the stairs, she stopped to glance back at him. He was looking at her with a worried frown.

"If you don't mind my saying so, Miss Joanna, you don't look well."

Even if she did mind, Halton would still say whatever he wanted, albeit in the most tactful way. Having worked for the Clooneys since she was ten, the butler was part of the family.

"I'm just tired. I'll be fine," she said, giving him a reassuring smile, and continued up the stairs. She didn't want to talk about it. Not now. Maybe never.

The hot shower washed away some of her exhaustion, but the ache inside remained. No amount of water could wash that away. Afterward she put on a thick terry robe and went out into the upper hallway.

As she walked toward the stairs she heard Halton's voice from the foyer below, unusually loud and insistent.

"I told you, sir, Miss Clooney is not at home."

"Then I'll wait."

Joanna's heart missed a beat. Reid? No, it couldn't be. She must be so overtired she was imagining things.

"I'm afraid that won't be possible," Halton said firmly. "You'll have to come back tomorrow, sir."

"Nothing doing, pal. I'm not leaving till I've spoken to Miss Clooney."

It wasn't her imagination. That *was* Reid's voice, with the granite edge she knew so well. Her legs felt stiff as she moved to the top of the staircase.

There he stood, in the hall below, scanning the empty living room through the open French doors.

"It's all right, Halton, I'll speak to Mr. O'Connor." Somehow her voice still worked, but the muscles in her throat constricted painfully as he turned to look up at her.

Now she knew how a deer felt, trapped in the glare of oncoming headlights. Never taking his glittering eyes from her face, Reid slowly crossed the hall to the foot of the stairs.

Joanna walked down to meet him, dimly aware that Halton had disappeared silently in the direction of the kitchen. Her thoughts whirled in turmoil. He must have come to let her know that her mother was all set for the summer. What else could it be?

The emptiness inside felt more acute than ever, but it had one positive side effect. She felt very calm. As she descended the stairs to the marble tiles of the foyer, she felt nothing.

She walked straight into the long, gracious living room and Reid followed. In the center of the room she stopped, turned to face him and waited for him to speak, to tell her why he had come.

"Aren't you going to ask me how your mother is?"

The criticism in his voice didn't bother her. What did his opinion matter?

She shrugged. "I assumed that's what you had come to tell me."

He dug into the pocket of his denim shirt, pulled out a small slip of paper and handed it to her. "Her phone number."

"Thanks." She took it from him and slipped it into the pocket of her robe without looking at it.

With his mission now accomplished, he could leave. But he just stood and looked at her with a steady, enigmatic scrutiny. What was he waiting for? She turned away, walked over to the window and stared blindly out toward the rose garden.

Behind her, he softly cleared his throat. "The first time you left me I never got a chance to see you, to speak to you. This time I was determined to have my say—"

"I never knew you came to see me," she broke in abruptly, turning her head to look at him. "I never saw any letters."

She couldn't stand the thought that he'd believed she'd refused to see him. Even at this late date, she wanted to set the record straight. Even though it meant exposing her father.

His eyes darkened, but otherwise his face remained impassive. "What would you have done if you'd known I came after you?" The little pulse beside his mouth began to beat and her heart kept time.

"I would have seen you." She could barely get the words out her throat hurt so much. "What were you going to say?"

An eternity seemed to pass while she waited for his answer. The room was quiet and still; even the ormolu clock on the mantel seemed to be holding its breath.

"I was going to say, 'Come back to me. I love you, with all my heart and all my soul.'" He looked her straight in the eye, but his expression remained unreadable and his voice quite steady.

"And now?" She struggled to keep her voice even, too, but the huskiness betrayed her tension. "What have you come all this way to tell me, now?"

Anxiously she searched his eyes for some clue to his feelings. They remained cool and impenetrable, almost serene. Despair filled her and she turned to stare out the window again. A man in love would not be so composed. She was being a fool, yet again.

"I don't know if what your mother said was true...." Suddenly his voice was low and unsteady, and her heart began beating much too fast. "I don't know if you could ever love me again, but I need to know for sure. Am I too late? Is it too late to ask for another chance?" He paused, as if speech were a struggle. "I've never stopped loving you, although I've spent the last three years wishing I could."

Words froze in her throat. What if this was just some cruel dream? She couldn't bear to turn and look at him for fear he would disappear before her very eyes. Then he moved, until he was standing very close behind her.

His warm breath stirred the damp hairs at the nape of her neck; the heat from his body burned through her terry robe to the bare skin beneath, making her tremble.

"Am I too late, Joanna?"

She quivered in response to his low, fervent words, but she needed more. Running her tongue over her dry lips, she closed her eyes. "You said that we were never in love, just sexually attracted, and that's why it didn't work before. What's so different this time?"

"I said a lot of stupid things." He sounded sad and regretful. "Our relationship wasn't just based on sex and you know it. Back then I wasn't ready to be married. I was insecure and anxious to prove my suitability. But I'm ready now. The only thing I feel the need to prove now is how much I love you."

Perhaps this was all some bizarre manifestation of her fevered brain. After all, there was only so much stress a human being could endure.

His hands curved around her upper arms, sending a ripple of excruciating need through her. Slowly, he turned her to face him. He looked down into her eyes, his expression so achingly intent and unsure that it turned her heart inside out. "I love you. I never wanted you to leave before. I can't bear the thought of your leaving me now."

"But what about your fiancée?" She stared up at him, dazed and still too afraid to think this could be real.

Looking faintly rueful, he let her go. Shoving his hands in his pockets, he turned away to face the window. "I don't have a fiancée."

She let out a tiny gasp. "I don't understand."

"I broke off the engagement right after I first saw you again."

She stared at him in disbelief. "Why?"

He turned back from the window with a sheepish shrug. "Because you can't marry someone when you're still in love with someone else. I only got engaged when I read about your engagement to Paul," he finished softly.

He was looking at her intently, his eyes glowing with a light she remembered so well, that brilliant warmth shining just for her. Her heart felt as if it would burst.

"What do say, Joanna?" The anxiety showed in his voice now. "Will you give me another chance? I promise I'll try to do better this time."

Not even in her wildest dreams had she ever allowed herself to imagine this happening, that she would be given a second chance. This time she wasn't going to blow it. But there were things she had to tell him.

"When I left you the first time, I never meant it to be forever. I never wanted to get a divorce."

"If you never meant to divorce me, why did you leave?" He gave her a searching look.

"I guess I needed some proof that you wanted me, that you loved me. But you never came after me. I took it as a sign that you just didn't care. There was no point in going back to a man who didn't love me."

For a moment he stared at her. Then his face cleared and his mouth curved into a smile of sheer gladness. "I've been such a fool. And you still haven't answered my question. Will you—"

"Yes!" She didn't give him a chance to finish. "Yes!"

She managed a breathless laugh before he gave a groan and pulled her urgently into his arms. The intense thankfulness and relief in that sound filled her with inexpressible warmth and the sheer bliss of belonging.

He pressed her tightly against him, one hand cradling her head. Hardly able to breathe, she buried her face in his chest, her senses flooded with the scent of him, the feel of him.

"I love you, I always have," she whispered, her arms tightening around him, overwhelmed with a happiness and joy that was almost more than she could bear. If she died now, she'd die happy. It still seemed utterly impossible, but miracles really did happen.

He lifted his head and looked down at her, his eyes bright with happiness. She raised her hands to his face, caressing the smooth curve of his jaw, trailing her thumbs across his lips in wonder.

A slow, triumphant smile curved his mouth under her fingertips. He bent his head and kissed her, a long, deep, famished kiss, and wrapped her tightly in his arms.

She opened her mouth wide to him, straining against him in a frenzy of need, as relief and happiness made her head spin. She wrapped her arms around him even tighter, loving the feeling of his hard, solid strength pressed so close, wanting to absorb him and be absorbed by him.

He broke the kiss to take a deep, ragged breath, then leaned his forehead against hers, still holding her tightly, desperately.

She snuggled against his chest as a rush of painful regret raced through her. "When I think of all the time we wasted. If I'd had even an inkling that you wanted me, I'd have been back in a flash."

Reid's voice was soft and husky. "We've both been fools."

He kissed her again, fiercely, almost roughly, but it inflamed her, made her body tighten and ache to be stroked by him, outside and in. She pressed her hips against him and he needed no other hint.

Wrenching his mouth away from hers he said, "Let's go upstairs."

She didn't need a second invitation. She took his hand and led the way out. In the hall they met Halton carrying a tray with a sandwich and a glass of milk.

"Put that in the fridge for me, Halton. I'll get it later," she said with a smile, as they continued up the stairs.

"Yes, miss," Halton said resignedly, but she caught his small approving smile.

Reid chuckled under his breath. Suddenly he swept her off her feet and into his arms, and took the stairs two at a time until they reached the second floor, where he stopped to open the door of her room.

"You remembered," she breathed as he carried her in and kicked the door shut behind him.

"Remembered! You've haunted my every waking moment." His voice was rough, his breathing labored as he lowered her to her feet.

Without wasting a second, he unfastened her robe and slipped it off her shoulders as he backed her toward the bed. Almost as soon as the robe hit the floor, his own clothing followed.

He laid her down on the soft covers, and lowered himself, hard and ready, between her thighs.

Supporting himself on his elbows, he looked down at her face. Beneath the glaze of desire, his eyes were still serious, the pain not quite obliterated. "I've had a chance to find out what life is like without you. And I'll never let you leave me again. You're mine, body and soul. And I'm yours. Right beside me is where you're going to stay."

"Ooh, I love it when you get masterful," she drawled, teasing him, but determined to wipe away every last trace of pain forever.

Her heart expanded in her chest until she was almost breathless. She felt so warm and secure and loved. This must be what heaven was like. And when Reid covered her mouth with his, she was sure of it.

Epilogue

"LIVE WITH YOU? You must be mad!"

Joanna blinked as her mother erupted in incredulous laughter.

"Don't you want to?" From her seat at the cottage dining table she shot Reid a baffled look as he came in from the kitchen with a bottle of champagne and some glasses.

They had driven up to give her mother the good news and make what Joanna considered a perfectly sensible suggestion. Reid shrugged indulgently at her mother's foibles and met her eyes with a loving warmth that filled her with happiness.

Across the table, her mother leaned back in the old wooden chair and shook her head. "No, I don't want to. I'm glad you two fools came to your senses, but if I had to watch you drool over each other every day I'd want to slip back into a coma again."

"But I don't like the thought of your living alone," Joanna protested, "and we don't mind, honestly we don't, so if that's what's stopping you—"

"It isn't. Thanks for the offer, but you kids need to be alone. As for me," she hastened to add, as Joanna opened her mouth to argue, "Thelma has agreed to stay with me as a companion. So you see, everything has worked out beautifully." She smiled over at the nurse sitting on the sofa, who nodded her agreement.

Joanna went over to her mother and bent down to enfold her in a loving hug. "Yes, it has, hasn't it? Thank you for being such a meddling old biddy."

"You're welcome, dear," her mother said complacently as she squeezed her back, then gave Joanna a broad grin as she straightened up. "What's a mother for? To love her children and help them solve their problems."

"You mean to interfere," Joanna said dryly.

Reid poured them each a glass of champagne and set the bottle on the table. After Thelma joined them in drinking a celebratory toast, he put down his glass and eyed her mother with an odd expression on his face. "You know, Louise, this might sound weird, but I visited you in the hospital, just a couple of weeks before you woke up. I went to see you because I had a problem."

He looked at Joanna a little sheepishly. "I'd just heard about your engagement. It hit me hard, the realization that all hope was gone. I decided that I might as well think about getting married myself. I wanted a family, and I wasn't getting any younger." He paused for a moment and looked at Louise. "I was confused, I needed to know if I was doing the right thing. And it's almost as if you heard me."

"Oh Reid, you're not saying my mother came out of her coma because . . ."

They looked at each other for a moment, then shook their heads. "No . . ."

"Oh ye of little faith!" Louise burst out. "Why is it so impossible to believe that a mother's love could transcend any obstacle?"

"Oh, Mom!" Joanna rolled her eyes and grinned, then linked her arm in Reid's. "Let's get out of here, before she starts demonstrating astral travel."

"Just remember, you've got me to thank for all this. Now run along and have fun. I'm sure you still have lots to talk over."

She winked at Thelma, and was dismayed to see that her companion had pulled a pristine cotton hanky from the pocket of her pink shirtwaist and was dabbing at her eyes.

She got up and went to her with a little frown of concern. "Thelma, you're not crying because I won the bet, are you?"

"What bet?" Joanna paused on her way to the door.

"Of course not. I was never so tickled to lose twenty bucks." Thelma sniffed and stuffed the handkerchief back in her pocket, obviously annoyed with herself for giving way.

"What bet?" Joanna asked again.

Her mother gave her an impatient look. "The bet we had on you and Reid."

"You had a bet on us?" Joanna stared at her, bemused and a little indignant.

"Why not? You were more fun than the horses." Louise put a comforting arm around her friend and hugged her tight. "If it's not the money, then why are you so upset?"

"I'm not upset. I just love a happy ending."

"Dear Thelma. You must remember that this isn't the end, it's just the beginning."

HARLEQUIN®

Temptation®

COMING NEXT MONTH

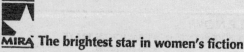

Women throughout time have
lost their hearts to:

Starting in January 1996, Harlequin Temptation
will introduce you to five irresistible, sexy rogues.
Rogues who have carved out their place in history,
but whose true destinies lie in the arms of
contemporary women.

#569 *The Cowboy,* Kristine Rolofson
(January 1996)

#577 *The Pirate,* Kate Hoffmann
(March 1996)

#585 *The Outlaw,* JoAnn Ross
(May 1996)

#593 *The Knight,* Sandy Steen
(July 1996)

#601 *The Highwayman,* Madeline Harper
(September 1996)

Dangerous to love, impossible to resist!

HARLEQUIN Temptation

Mail Order Men—Satisfaction Guaranteed!

Texas Man 2—Ben Bradley

This sexy rancher is six foot two, lean and muscular. He loves his land, horses and women—although not necessarily in that order.

Ben doesn't want or need a wife, so when his matchmaking mother puts his profile into *Texas Men* magazine he is not pleased. But when his mother bets him the neighbor's prize bull that she can find the "perfect woman," he undertakes the challenge.

Little does Ben realize that the "perfect woman" is right under his nose.

#604 THE TEXAN TAKES A WIFE
by Kristine Rolofson

Available in September wherever Harlequin books are sold.

HARLEQUIN Temptation

HARLEQUIN®

Don't miss these Harlequin favorites by some of our most
distinguished authors!
And now, you can receive a discount by ordering two or more titles!

HT #25663	THE LAWMAN by Vicki Lewis Thompson	$3.25 U.S.☐/$3.75 CAN. ☐
HP #11788	THE SISTER SWAP by Susan Napier	$3.25 U.S.☐/$3.75 CAN. ☐
HR #03293	THE MAN WHO CAME FOR CHRISTMAS by Bethany Campbell	$2.99 U.S.☐/$3.50 CAN. ☐
HS #70667	FATHERS & OTHER STRANGERS by Evelyn Crowe	$3.75 U.S.☐/$4.25 CAN. ☐
HI #22198	MURDER BY THE BOOK by Margaret St. George	$2.89 ☐
HAR #16520	THE ADVENTURESS by M.J. Rodgers	$3.50 U.S.☐/$3.99 CAN. ☐
HH #28885	DESERT ROGUE by Erin Yorke	$4.50 U.S.☐/$4.99 CAN. ☐

(limited quantities available on certain titles)

	AMOUNT	$
DEDUCT:	10% DISCOUNT FOR 2+ BOOKS	$
ADD:	POSTAGE & HANDLING	$
	($1.00 for one book, 50¢ for each additional)	
	APPLICABLE TAXES**	$_____
	TOTAL PAYABLE	$_____
	(check or money order—please do not send cash)	

To order, complete this form and send it, along with a check or money order for the
total above, payable to Harlequin Books, to: **In the U.S.:** 3010 Walden Avenue,
P.O. Box 9047, Buffalo, NY 14269-9047; **In Canada:** P.O. Box 613, Fort Erie, Ontario,
L2A 5X3.

Name: _____

Address: _____ City: _____

State/Prov.: _____ Zip/Postal Code: _____

**New York residents remit applicable sales taxes.
Canadian residents remit applicable GST and provincial taxes.   HBACK-JS3

Look us up on-line at: http://www.romance.net

By the Bestselling Author of
Romancing the Stone

CATHERINE LANIGAN

One man, three women

DANGEROUS *Love*

Richard Bartlow was a man people noticed. He was ruthless, sexy, ambitious and charming. In short, he was dangerous. Three women know only too well *how* dangerous.

Mary Grace—She lost everything when Richard suddenly left her and their children.
Alicia—She put her own life on hold to help Richard get his back on track.
Michelle—She mistakenly believed that she and Richard were destined to be together.

Find out how it all unravels this August at your favorite retail outlet.

REBECCA

43 LIGHT STREET

YORK

FACE TO FACE

Bestselling author Rebecca York returns to "43 Light Street"
for an original story of past secrets, deadly deceptions—and
the most intimate betrayal.

She woke in a hospital—with amnesia...and with child.
According to her rescuer, whose striking face is the last
image she remembers, she's Justine Hollingsworth. But
nothing about her life seems to fit, except for the baby
inside her and Mike Lancer's arms around her. Consumed
by forbidden passion and racked by nameless fear, she
must discover if she is Justine...or the victim of some mind
game. Her life—and her unborn child's—depends on it....

Don't miss *Face To Face*—Available in October, wherever
Harlequin books are sold.

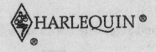

HARLEQUIN ®

®

43FTF

When all the evidence points to love,
there's only one verdict.

VERDICT:
Matrimony

Witness the power of love this September as
seasoned courtroom lawyers discover that
sometimes there's just no defense against love.

This special collection of three complete stories
by your favorite authors makes a compelling
case for love.

WITHOUT PRECEDENT by JoAnn Ross
VOICES IN THE WIND by Sandra Canfield
A LEGAL AFFAIR by Bobby Hutchinson

Available this September wherever Harlequin
and Silhouette books are sold.

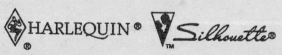